**THANK YOU** so much for buying this book!

As a way of showing gratitude, I wanted to extend a very special offer to you. I'm giving selected readers access to my **VIP Mailing List**. As part of this group, you will receive notifications about promotions and new releases!

Do you want to read more romance stories full of **Adventures**, **Passion,** and **Emotions** every week?

Go to http://eepurl.com/cMCM_D to join today!

# Blizzard

## Savage Brotherhood MC: Book Two

## A Paranormal Romance

By Jasmine Wylder

# Chapter One

*Shadow*

Lots of the boys in the gang liked to ride their bikes loud. Obnoxious, screaming at everybody to look at them and be amazed and intimidated. They were a bunch of idiots looking to compensate for small brains and small dicks. Val liked her bike smooth. Understated. You didn't know it was there until it was already past you. Just like her.

This morning, though, she could have used a little noise. Val scowled as she pulled her bike up next to the blue-gray minivan parked outside her brother's house. The guy she'd picked out at the bar last time to take up into the woods had turned out to be a colossal disappointment. All muscle, big and sexy, but with no idea how to treat a woman right. She'd have done better by herself. Then he had the nerve to act as though she should have pretended to enjoy him!

Grumbling under her breath, Val turned off her bike and took off her helmet. Her leather jacket fit snugly around her curvy frame, nipping in at her waist to accentuate her shape. She flipped her braids over her shoulder and ran a hand over the shorter half of her head. It was getting a little long for her tastes. Should she buzz it or just shave it all off?

The chatter of voices brought her out of her darker thoughts and Val quickly jogged around the house. Her heart burst into sunlight as she saw her brother with his mate, Ava, pushing a stroller with their infant daughter, Lily, in it. Behind them were three tow-headed girls.

"Mama!" The youngest, four-year-old Freya, shouted as she rushed to Val's arms.

Val caught her and kissed the top of her head. Her leopard rumbled with happiness, curled up tight in her chest. She was always happy to be reunited with her daughters after spending time apart. Her older two, ten-year-old Artemis and six-year-old Sekhmet, joined in the hug. Sekhmet started to excitedly tell her that she had found a fossil, while Artemis snorted and rolled her eyes. Val shot her oldest a warning look and Artemis shrugged.

"Are you three ready to go home?" Val asked, smiling at her daughters. "Have you had lunch yet?"

Freya bounced on her toes. “Nope! Can we go to Les’s bar?”

Val didn’t miss Ava’s disapproving look, but at this time of day the bar would be mostly empty, and the food was good. Besides, the gang knew better than to try to smoke or drink around her girls. “Sure we can, honey. Go get in the van. Sekhmet, Artemis, no fighting.”

“Yes, Mama,” they agreed happily and raced for the minivan.

Val hated the vehicle, but safety came first when it came to her daughters. She turned to Ava and Jackson. “Thanks for watching them.”

“It’s always a joy to have them around,” Ava assured her as Jackson grinned broadly.

Val nodded. Not for the first time, she was glad that Jackson had ignored her advice when the vampire king, Astrophel, had decided to claim Ava. Val had been all about handing her over, letting the vampires kill her. She hadn't thought that the panther shifter was worth the fight. As it turned out, though, she was, and Val was glad that she was around. Jackson had never been happier since Ava came into his life.

Artemis and Sekhmet were arguing over the validity of Sekhmet's 'fossils' by the time Val put her bike in the back of the van and got into the driver's seat herself. She allowed it to go on for a moment, waiting for them to come to a conclusion on their own, before she spoke.

"Enough, you two. Or you'll have to clean the bathroom together when you get home." She looked seriously in the rearview mirror until she was satisfied that they weren't going to fight anymore, then pulled away. She waved to Jackson and Ava and then turned her attention to the road. "After lunch, do you want to go to the museum?"

"Yeah!" Artemis leaned forward, her eyes bright and excited. "They have a new exhibit on the local Native nation and I want to see the canoe!"

"I want to see the dollies," Freya shouted.

Sekhmet kicked the back of Val's seat. "Fossils!"

Val felt herself relaxing, far better than she had been able to with her orgasm-less sex spree last night. The gang had been having a bit of trouble lately. Since Astrophel's death, the local vampires had been without a leader. It meant that they were fighting each other to become the new king, which led to fewer vampires straying into Savage Brotherhood territory. This, in turn, led to the gang having less to do and getting bored. Boredom made them restless and restlessness turned them all into a bunch of idiots. They'd been pulling jobs all over town, from robberies to vandalism, meaning that the long arm of the law was coming down harder on them.

If they didn't start shaping up, Val might end up having to claw a few throats out as a lesson to the others.

She shook those thoughts off, determined to enjoy spending time with her girls, when red and blue lights started flashing behind her. Her leopard snarled as her shoulders bunched. Speaking of the long arm of the law...

It was the sheriff's car. Gabriel Cunningham. Mr. Holier-than-thou himself. A snarl ripped from her this time, her nostrils flaring. A quick glance at her odometer showed her well within the accepted speed range. If her daughters weren't in the van, she might have been tempted to try to book it out of there. Instead, she pulled off to the side of the road and unbuckled.

"Stay in your seats," she told the girls and then stepped out of the van.

If it wasn't Gabriel, she'd have stayed put and tried to talk her way out of whatever the cop wanted. Him though... the traitor had better have a good reason for showing his face.

Gabriel stepped from his car and her leopard let out a hiss—part anger, part desire. Even though he was getting up there in years, his body was still built like a brick shit house. Broad shoulders, muscled chest that stretched the fabric of his uniform, rock-hard abs. His square jaw was set in anger and his eyes hidden behind mirrored glasses. His salt-and-pepper hair was shorn down to a length somewhere between too long and too short.

"What do you want, Blizzard?"

She could have kicked herself for calling him by his old nickname. He didn't deserve it anymore. Not when he abandoned the gang for the military, only to come back and become the fucking sheriff. The old tattoos from when they used to pull jobs together seemed to burn on her shoulders. Did his matching tats have the same effect on him? She glowered at him as he got closer.

"Do you have to do this every time I pull you over?" Gabriel took off his glasses to sneer at her. "You're supposed to stay in your vehicle when you're pulled over."

"Fuck you," she snarled, the familiar burn of hatred clouding her mind. "You have no right to come after me when I have my girls with me."

A startled look came over Gabriel's features. He glanced at the van, his expression turning worried for a moment, before it hardened again. "Maybe you shouldn't run around being a criminal if you don't want them to see you get arrested."

"Arrested?" What had she done recently to get on good ol' Gabe's list? Maybe preventing that idiot Basil from doing some home invasions.

"I'll let you drop them off with your brother if you promise to come quietly afterward."

The bastard. Val glowered at him, every muscle in her body tense. She rolled to the balls of her feet, preparing to spring toward him and rip his throat out. If he thought that he was going to separate her from her girls, he had another thing coming. And using them to make her cooperate?

"What are you planning to do, Gabe? What are you trying to arrest me for? What happened to our agreement?"

The gang handled the vampires and kept a low profile, Gabriel looked the other way. That was the arrangement they had. If he had decided to go back on it, then there would be bloodshed. If he started arresting gang members, especially the alpha's sister, then what was the point in sticking to the shadows? They'd be running amuck in no time.

Gabriel narrowed his eyes and lifted his lip. The smell of wolf on him increased, pulling something in her core. Dammit, why did he had to affect her like this when she already wanted to kill him?

"I got some things I want to talk to you about, Val. It doesn't have to be an arrest... yet. Let's just take this calmly and talk down at the station."

"Not unless you give me a good reason."

His dark eyes drilled into hers. The one thing that terrified her most about Gabriel Cunningham was that she never knew what he was thinking. Val could read people. It's what she did. He was like a brick wall.

Finally, he snorted. "I received an anonymous tip that you've been selling cocaine. I'm not about to let this town become a haven for drug pushers."

Val snarled, raising her fists. He knew nothing. "Why do you think I'd end up in drugs, Cunningham? These anonymous tips—ever stop to think maybe you should have evidence?"

"I do have evidence," Gabriel hissed. His eyes blazed as he stepped forward, looming over her as though that was intimidating. "I've got pictures,

Val. What are you thinking? Have you gotten hooked?"

If it was anybody else, she'd think he was actually concerned. But not Gabe. Not this traitor who turned his back on them all just because he couldn't be alpha—she remembered the scent of blood in the air as he and Jackson fought. The way muscles were torn open, cut to the bone. Her leopard crouched, ready to pounce.

"Are you sure of that?" she hissed at him, then relaxed her stance enough so that when she reached to undo the top button of his shirt, he didn't immediately grab her wrists. "Or are you just wanting me in a prison cell, helpless to your oceans of lust?"

He smacked away her hand. “I have enough evidence to take your girls away if you don’t cooperate.”

She didn’t think as she seized him around the throat. “Try it and I’ll kill you.”

Her leopard paced anxiously, teeth bared and on edge. All her muscles trembled as the taste of blood burned sour in the back of her throat. Her chest heaved, and a red mist started to encroach on the edges of her vision. Her fangs dropped, ready to tear apart the enemy before her.

“Easy.” Gabriel’s voice was a familiar soft purr now. “You’re going into berserker mode. You don’t want your girls to see that.”

He was right.

Val forced herself to release him and exhaled noisily. As she inhaled again, trying to clear her mind, she caught the whiff of a sweet, pungent odor. Like rotten fruit. Her head whipped around, but it was too late. A tall, thin and pale person plunged through the trees and knocked into her. She went flying. The vampire landed on her, its fangs flashing in the sunlight, as long fingers wrapped around her throat.

Vampires. In daylight.

Val shifted in the blink of an eye, bringing her Leopard forward. The vampire screeched as she twisted out of its grip. Claws raked across her back, but she turned and sunk her teeth into its withered neck. She thrashed the body from side to side, grinning as she felt bone snap. Tossing the vampire's body aside, she turned again. Gabriel in wolf form faced off with two vampires.

A third yanked open the doors to the minivan. Screams filled the air and she heard Artemis shout for the others to get back.

Red washed over her vision. Everything disappeared around her, except for the scent of rotten fruit. She dashed forward, a roar in her throat as she collided with the vampire. Teeth in throat. Taste of blood. Crushed flesh in her jaws. Screams of pain. She could sense her girls, huddled in the van. In danger. Claws dug into muscle. Head ripped off.

A howl behind her. She lunged. Teeth caught on dry skin. The stench of rot strong in her nose. Rip chest open. Tear out heart. Taste of blood.

Everything red around her. Need for more. Lips dripping with spit. Scent of wolf. Enemy. She leapt and came down. Knocked him to the ground. Teeth tear at the throat. Blocked. Arm. She yanked her head to the side. Clawed at the throat. Blocked.

Freya was crying. Sobbing. Sekhmet whimpering. Artemis calling for her.

The red started to fade. The enemy beneath her, the man whose blood was in her mouth, wasn't fighting her back. Her claws dug into his shoulder, but she slowly pulled them back. Everything crashed down around her. Light, sound, color, as though she had been in a dark tub of water and was suddenly born into the world.

"Easy, now. It's okay."

She looked down to find Gabriel in human form staring up at her. His arm was clenched tight in her jaws, blood pouring from his shoulder where her claws had ripped into him. His brown eyes burned into her, frightened but in control.

"There you are, Sweetness. Come back to us now. The vampires are gone. Your girls are safe. Come on, Shadow. Shake it off."

Slowly, she released him. The lingering adrenaline left her on edge, ready to lunge for his throat if he made the wrong move. Her leopard snarled, then whined. Val allowed herself to shift back into her human form. Release the berserker. As soon as it was her hands and not paws pressed into Gabriel's chest, he bucked his body. Val yelped as he threw her off. She lashed out, but he grabbed both her arms and twisted them behind her back and pinned her down.

Her leopard huffed and stretched. The excitement of blood had left it frisky and it wanted to mate. Now. As Gabriel pinned her down with his body.

“Easy,” he grunted and reached for the ruined remnants of his uniform. Her own clothes were torn to shreds from her shift. He snapped a pair of cuffs on her.

“Let me go,” she snarled. “I have to tell Jackson about this! Vampires! Attacking in daylight! How could they—”

“Yeah. And you went into berserker mode, Val. I thought you had a better handle on it than that. What if you had hurt your daughters?”

Val screamed in fury. How dare he suggest that she might hurt them?

"You can explain to Jackson at the station." Gabriel yanked her to her feet. The glare was heavy on his brow as he pushed her toward her van. "You got extra clothes?"

She snarled.

"I'll take that as a no. Sit quietly." He pushed her to the minivan and shoved her in the front seat. "I'll be back in a minute."

Val closed her eyes as he walked away. A headache pounded through her brain as she slowly returned more fully to herself. She was aware that her girls were all crying now and her heart nearly broke. She took a deep breath and twisted around to look at them.

“Are you hurt?”

Artemis clutched Freya in her arms and shook her head. Her eyes were wide, while Sekhmet huddled in the back. The fear on their faces made Val want to shrivel up and die. Tears burned her eyes, though she would not let them fall. Back at his car, she saw Gabriel dressing in a spare uniform, as well as gathering up the ruined clothes. The vampires had turned to dust—like they ought to in sunlight.

Val slumped back in her seat and closed her eyes. What the fuck had just happened?

# Chapter Two

*Blizzard*

The orange jumpsuit was just a little too small for her, but it was better than being naked. Gabriel kept his eyes on his task, gently wiping the dried blood from where it had run down Val's arm. The wound, a long but shallow scratch, wasn't enough to require a doctor. When he started to clean it with an alcohol wipe, Val jumped, hissed and spat at him. He tensed, ready for an attack, but then she sagged back against the wall.

Her bright eyes remained locked on him, wary and mistrustful. Gabriel snorted. His wolf paced in his chest, snarling quietly. After the way she had gone after him earlier, his wolf wanted to subdue her, make her kneel and ensure she would never be a threat again.

But Valarie Masters would always be a threat.

“Stop glaring at me as though you want to claw out my eyes,” he spat at her. His arm burned from where she had sunk her teeth into him. He’d have to put on new bandages once he had her patched up. “Unless you want me to send you to the hospital?”

She hissed again, but turned her face away. The jail cells in the Coalfell police station were small, too small for a shifter to comfortably be in. He had thought that was a good thing when he first became sheriff. Now, though, he wondered if he could find it in the budget to expand a little.

Val's gaze was on the door outside, but her eyes were unfocused. As he pressed gauze to her wound, some of the fierceness faded away. He couldn't help but sneak glances at her face. If she knew how beautiful he found her, she'd probably rip out his jugular. But she was beautiful. All curves from head to toe. Shoulders nearly as broad as his. Even the way she did her hair, half shaven, the other half in braids, was beautiful. Silver rings winked from where they ran up one ear. She looked like a wild warrior-queen.

"You've got a new tattoo," he noted, turning her arm over. A black lily stood out vividly against her pale skin.

"Eyes up," she grunted at him.

"For your niece?"

"Is this a jail cell or a tea party?"

Gabriel ground his teeth. What did he care about her tattoos? She was a brash, rude and altogether too violent woman to be left out on the streets. He had the evidence he needed to lock her up forever. His town would be much better off for it.

"You and the gang are going off-kilter," he told her bluntly. "Drugs, Val? What the hell are you thinking? Jackson's never allowed drugs in Coalfell. Are you dealing behind his back?"

"Don't worry about my brother's back. I've got it." Val turned her glare back on him. For a moment, he thought that was going to be it, then she shrugged and held out her other arm, which was ripped up nastily as well. As he started cleaning it up, she spoke again, her voice low. "There's been a lot of stuff going on. The guys are bored and getting themselves into trouble, which has opened up Coalfell to another gang. Don't know who they are yet, but they're selling dirty drugs."

"All drugs are dirty."

Val snorted. "I guess that's the difference between us, eh? I'd rather see people keep going on pure stuff than see them die horrible deaths because their supply was contaminated."

She was right about that, but he didn't want to admit it. So he wiped off a long cut more roughly than necessary and snapped, "Guess the money you get from it doesn't hurt, either?"

Her eyes yellowed and he grabbed her wrists, making sure that she couldn't attack him. In response, Val twisted and kneed toward his groin. He was only just able to maneuver them both so she was pinned down, unable to hurt him. The hatred in her eyes made his wolf snarl. Then she threw one leg over his hip, thrusting her pelvis to his.

His wolf immediately sung a different tune.

"Stop that," he snapped at her, putting distance between them. He wasn't some sex-starved pup who'd let himself get seduced by a criminal.

"Then get your fucking hands off me."

Gabriel drew back. He grabbed the first aid kit and threw it at her. "Lick your own wounds, then."

He stomped out of the cell before she could turn his choice of words against him.

Why did she have to be like that? He slammed the door behind him. She was the most infuriating woman he'd ever met. If she was ten years younger he'd blame it on her being an irrational teenager, but she hadn't been a teen for a long time. It was just her personality. Contrary, rude and impossible. She'd bite the hand that fed her clean off.

He stomped his way to the break room, where one of his deputies sat with Val's three girls. They all eyed him with the same distrust their mother had. Something in his chest twisted. There was a time, when Artemis was just a baby, that he was one of the few people that Val trusted to leave her with. But that was back when her parents were alive. Before Jackson became alpha of the local chapter.

He attempted to smooth out his expression when he addressed them. “Your uncle should be here soon to pick you up. Do you—”

“Are those bad men coming back for Mama?” the littlest looked at him with wide eyes, the same brown as Val’s. They all looked exactly like her, except for their blonde hair, while she was a brunette. “Are you’s gonna fight them?”

How much did they know about what the Brotherhood did against vampires? Gabriel stared at her for a moment, uncertain of how to respond to that, when he heard a bellow in the main area of the station. He gestured for the deputy to stay where she was, then went to face Jackson Masters. He’d earned the nickname Tornado well—he came in like a devil and was wildly unpredictable. Smart, though, which made him a good alpha.

"The hell, Cunningham?" Tornado snarled at him.

Gabriel rolled his eyes. Speechless with rage, it seemed. "Was there a question in that, Masters?"

"Let my sister go this minute or so help me—"

Ava spoke behind him. "Jackson!"

Gabriel tilted his head to get a look at her. She grabbed her mate's arm and gave him a warning glare. Gabriel repressed the urge to grin at that. He never thought he'd see the day when Jackson Masters got whipped, but this little woman had done the job masterfully. Jackson made a low growling noise, but when Ava narrowed her eyes further he nodded.

"Where are the girls?" Ava asked.

Gabriel gestured. "I'm sure they're going to have lots of questions for you."

Ava's black glare turned on him now. She stomped into the break room, leaving the two men alone. Jackson opened his mouth, then closed it again. When the girls came out, his stance softened. He quickly moved to them, asking each one if she was alright.

"Take them home to Lily," Jackson murmured to Ava. "I'm going to be a while."

Ava nodded as she pressed herself to her toes to kiss him. "Don't be an idiot."

Gabriel snickered. With one last glare, Ava and the girls left. The deputy exited the break room looking wary, and he gestured her away. “Go do a patrol, Katie. I’ve got this.”

Katie frowned a moment, but nodded. She knew about the agreement he had with Tornado, having been attacked by vampires herself. She was the only survivor of her entire family and backed him up whenever she could. It helped that he had been the one to save her life.

Once Katie was gone, Gabriel sat in his office chair. Tornado remained standing, looking even more murderous than he had before.

“What the hell are you doing, Cunningham?”

“Charging Valarie with drug possession and dealing. I’ve got all the evidence that I need.”

Tornado’s lips pulled back in a snarl. “That’s not our deal.”

“Not going to deny that you’ve pulled the gang into drugs, then? Your parents would be ashamed of you.”

Tornado’s hands slammed against the desk, but Gabriel didn’t flinch. “Don’t you dare talk about my parents as though you care about what they wanted for the gang. They wanted me to be alpha, but that didn’t stop you from trying to tear out my throat for the position yourself.”

Gabriel’s wince took him by surprise. That wound had long closed over, hadn’t it? “Our deal is that if you don’t control the vampires, your gang is doing no good and I'll bring you down. Well, there have been three murders in the past four months that are directly linked to vampire activity. Not to mention that you failed to tell me that now they're running around in daylight!"

"Daylight?" Tornado's eyes widened. "What… How?"

So he hadn't known. It didn't soften Gabriel toward him at all. "You should know that, Masters. As Alpha, you should know that before they start attacking your sister and nieces."

Tornado's knees buckled. His face went white as he clutched the edge of the desk. His head fell to his chest. For a long moment, he stood like that and Gabriel waited. Perhaps it had been a low blow, but he had to understand what he was up against.

Finally, Tornado looked up. “We’ve got word that there’s a new king. Don’t know who it is yet, but he’s been very aggressive. So far, it’s only been toward gang members. No deaths outside of vamp territory, not around here, at least, but in Ivywood they’re having real problems. The thing is that the murders have only happened in daytime. Thunder thought the new king was bribing humans to do the job, but if vamps are walking around in daylight… that changes everything.”

“And something like that is something I need to know, Masters.” Gabriel leaned forward in his chair, his wolf urging him to take the pup by the throat and put him down. “Before it gets to the point where Shadow’s gone berserker, I'm still booking her on the drug charges."

Jackson growled.

"Don't give me that. You know the rules. I come down on you when there are deaths involved. Drugs kill. "

"I want to talk to her."

"Not happening, Masters." Tornado started to growl again, and Gabriel got to his feet. "Do you really want to push it? We both know that if this comes to a fight, one of us is dying. If it's me, you won't be far behind. Death or life in jail. Is that the kind of father you want to be to your little girl?"

Tornado growled again but Gabriel saw his words had the desired effect. He turned on his heel and walked away without another word.

***

Several hours later, while Katie was still out on patrol and Gabriel was staring at the unfinished paperwork he needed to send in to make Val's arrest official, the door to the station opened. He looked up sharply, hand immediately going to the gun at his side. He frowned when he saw who it was. Melanie Seymour, wearing her waitress uniform.

"What are you doing here?" he hissed at once. Tornado was certain to have people watching the station. If they realized that Melanie was the one giving him information about their new drug dealing, she was done for.

"I'm here because you're not doing your job," she shouted at him. Her hands bunched at her sides. Soft brown hair curled around her shoulders and her eyes shone brightly with tears. “One of my co-workers is in the hospital, overdosed! I *saw* that gangster leaving here. Why haven’t you arrested him?”

Gabriel shot a look at the cells. The way Melanie was shouting, there was no way that Val couldn’t hear her. If she didn’t stop, things could get very ugly for her, fast. “Miss Seymour, I need you to be quiet.”

“Don’t tell me to be quiet! This has gone on long enough. People are having their lives ruined because of this. If you don’t do anything about it—”

“I am doing something about it. I’ve got one of the gang members in a cell right now,” Gabriel growled at her. “If you don’t stop shouting, she’ll be able to identify you. Do you want them coming after you?”

Melanie's face paled at that, but it didn't stop her. “I have lived in this town my whole life. I know that the cops have never done anything about that gang. If you don’t—”

“I *am.*” Gabriel started to explain once more that he made an arrest, but before he finished, the door to the cells swung open.

Val, looking like she owned the place, in tight jeans and a tank that showed off bounteous cleavage, yawned as she sashayed in. Her gaze focused on Melanie, who suddenly got very quiet and very pale. Val grinned like a cat about to make a kill.

“So, you’re the little bitch who thinks she can cross the Brotherhood,” Val sneered. “Huh. You’re lucky that you’re Ava’s friend. You’d better scram before your luck runs out, little pussycat."

Gabriel moved between them. Even as he did, Melanie let out a frightened squeak and fled the station. Val laughed. Gabriel narrowed his eyes at her, one hand on his gun. This was bad, the gang knowing who his informant was... If Melanie was Ava's friend, though, it gave her a certain measure of protection. As long as she didn't push too hard.

"How did you get out of your cell?"

Val smirked. "You left it unlocked."

"No, I—" Shit. After he had thrown the first aid kit at her.

He reached for his cuffs, but Val was too fast. She crossed the space between them and head-butted him. Black and white spots whirled in front of his vision. He reached out to grab her and his hand landed on something soft, velvety—Val knocked his feet out from under him and pinned his hands with one hand while she snapped the cuffs on him with the other. Gabriel groaned as he shook himself.

"That was easier than I thought it would be," Val purred. She propped herself on her elbows over him as he glared at her. He wanted to tear off her head, he wanted—wait.

No.

That wasn't what his wolf wanted at all.

Her body pressed against his, those velvety curves snug against him. He yanked his hands, wanting to touch her, only for them to yank the desk. Gabriel twisted to see that she had looped the cuffs through the desk leg, effectively pinning him in place.

"See you, Cunningham."

The heat of her body left his. Her gaze trailed down his form for a moment and smirked when she got to the tent in his pants. Gabriel snarled, but it wasn't as vicious as he would have liked. With a laugh, Val left the station, her hips swaying hypnotically with every step.

"Shit," Gabriel muttered once she was gone.

Clearly, he needed a hookup. It was the only reason why his body would react in this way. How long had it been since he last had sex? A week? More? If Val could throw him down and get that reaction, it was clear he had some oats that needed sewing.

He yanked at the desk leg, but it was bolted to the floor. He yanked again—he wasn't going to let Katie come back and see him like this!

# Chapter Three

*Shadow*

Val made sure she was well in the clear before she stopped to check her phone messages. The first thing she noticed was a string of texts and missed calls from Ava and then finally, one from Jackson. She looked at that one first.

*Leave Melanie alone.*

Sure enough, the texts from Ava followed a similar vein. All panicked messages that were ill-disguised fears for her friend's life. Val snorted as she stuffed the phone into her pocket. Cunningham. What had he said to make her sister-in-law think she was going to kill off her best friend? Sure, Melanie had to be handled, but it wasn't like murder was first on the list.

Shaking her head, Val stomped into the strip club where Melanie worked after she got off from the cafe. She found herself a booth and ordered a shot of whiskey. A smile curled her lip as she saw that the other feline shifter was already on the stage, her curves wiggling as she danced on a pole. Val had to admit, the girl knew how to move that body of hers. It was times like this when Val wished she was a lesbian, or bi or... Basically, if she was attracted to women instead of, or as well as, men, it would certainly make life a lot easier...

Melanie made a swooping motion that caused her breasts to nearly fall out of her small, sequined bra. As she came up, wrapping her hands in her own hair, she caught sight of Val. Instantly, she froze. Val's drink came, and she toasted Melanie before downing it. Then she turned her attention to the small back room, where she knew Melanie's boss, Rodger, would be. He'd have noticed she was here by now.

A sick feeling twisted her stomach, not at all related to the alcohol she had just downed. Maybe it wasn't her attraction to men that was the problem, but rather the type of man that she fell for. They were either total scumbags or...

Her leopard stretched and batted her chest, telling her to go back to the police station and throw herself all over Gabriel Cunningham. It wasn't the first time she'd felt drawn to him. Back when he was part of the gang, she hadn't bothered being subtle when flirting with him. He always treated her like a kid, because she was, but she wasn't a kid anymore. The problem was, she could see herself doing a 'forever' kind of mistake with Cunningham.

He was all wrong for her. Or rather, she was all wrong for him. He'd proven that. Leaving the gang, joining the military. Honorably discharged and immediately back in Coalfell getting himself hired as sheriff. What was with that man?

If he came after her again, though, she'd kill him. For real this time. Nobody threatened what was hers and lived to tell the tale. There were plenty of bodies in the ground that proved that. She was the gang's enforcer for a reason, after all. When dirty work needed done, busted kneecaps, a bullet in the brain, Jackson knew where to turn. She'd get the job done quickly and cleanly.

Cunningham was enforcer before he quit. He knew exactly what it was like to have this job.

Val waved for another whiskey, scowling heavily. The stuff here wouldn't get her as buzzed as she'd like, but she couldn't go to Les's bar. Not yet.

Melanie's song ended, and she dashed into the back, as though she was the reason Val had come. No, she had overheard Melanie's hysterical screaming to Cunningham—a coworker overdosed. Val doubted that it was one of her waitress coworkers. That place barely paid their workers enough to pay rent, let alone buy drugs. No, here, among women who were desperate, bored, or broken, was where she'd get a lead.

Once she traced the tainted drugs back to their source, those dealers would learn what it meant to encroach on Savage Brotherhood territory. It would be a bloodbath. Something the berserker in her leopard looked forward to.

One of the servers brought her a note. Val flipped it open, emptied her second shot and headed for the back. Her lips curled back at the strong scent of bear as she did. Rodger was built like his animal. Huge, muscled from head to toe, with thick curly hair and heavy jaw. He grinned at her as she shut the door to his office behind her.

When she first met him, he was all charm and charisma. She hadn't known then that it was the charm of a snake oil salesman. Not until he turned her out on her ass for refusing to get an abortion.

Her skin crawled as he grinned at her.

“Shadow. It’s been a while. What brings you to my humble club?”

Val yawned, making sure that her fangs showed.

Rodger’s smile faded at once. “Not in the mood for chit-chat, I see. You haven’t changed one bit. Alright. You’re here about the drugs.”

“Yup.”

He hesitated a moment before scratching behind his left ear, something he only did when he was nervous. “I must have bought a bad batch. One of my girls, she ended up in the hospital. It wasn’t an overdose.”

"Imagine that." Val let a claw lengthen and started to clean under her nail.

Rodger stood. He paced for a moment before turning back to her. "Okay. So I bought from outside the Brotherhood. It was cheaper. Clearly a bad move. If you're here to kill me, do it. If you're not, then let's talk about striking up a new business arrangement."

The sudden gleam in his eyes made her skin crawl even worse. She forced herself to remain calm, though. She stood, moving to his private store of liquor. Ah. There we go. She pulled out a bottle of black cherry wine. His personal favorite, stuff he had imported all the way from Italy. Val poured herself a large tumbler full.

"Tell you what. I'll let you keep going at our previous rates... in exchange for some information."

Rodger moved up behind her. One of his large hands planted on her ass while he reached around to take the bottle of wine. "Always about business, aren't you?"

She snarled. "Remove your hand."

"Your talents are wasted on that sorry sap of a brother. I remember where your true talents lie. If you ever feel like coming back to work, I've got a place open for you. Always." His breath wafted across her neck.

The familiarity of this situation made her freeze. She'd come to Rodger when she was a new single mom, Artemis just a baby, looking for a way to get clean. Leave the gang life behind her and have a proper family life for her kid. And here, in this office, she had ended up doing things that she regretted, things that left her feeling sick of herself, far more than anything she'd done for the gang.

"You remember the great times we had, Valarie?" Rodger kissed her neck lightly. "I don't even care that you went and got yourself knocked up anymore. We'd make sure that doesn't happen again."

His arm wrapped around her waist and spun her toward the desk. She knew what he intended; pin her down, yank her pants off and have his way with her. Wasn't that how Sekhmet was conceived? When he told her that he'd give her a double bonus if she just submitted to him. So, she had. At the time, she had even convinced herself that she wanted it. He was charming, he was attractive.

And she wasn't a scared, naive kid anymore.

Snarling, Val twisted out of his grasp. She smashed her glass into his face, then grabbed both his arms and yanked them behind his back. Rodger let out a hiss of mingled surprise and pain. Val threw him face-down on the desk and crawled over him, pressing a knee painfully into the back of his neck. He grunted, struggling uselessly.

"I'm not a struggling eighteen-year-old girl you can take advantage of anymore, *bear*."

"Take advantage? Please! You practically begged me to fuck you." Rodger growled, but it trailed off to a hiss. “Your daddy complex isn’t my fault.”

Val grabbed one of his hands and twisted sharply until she felt bone snap. Rodger screamed, sweat breaking out over his face. She returned to her previous position, keeping him pinned. “Let’s try these business negotiations again, shall we? You tell me who your supplier is, I don’t kill you.”

Rodger hissed again. “I never met the guy. I got some stuff dropped off, then a call promising more at half the price you Savages charge. He even dropped off more upfront. I just had to leave the money in the park the next day.”

“And you didn’t think that was suspicious?” Val cursed under her breath, but released him. Rodger straightened, cradling his broken wrist to his chest. He flinched when Val stepped closer. “I find you’ve been pushing dirty drugs on these women again and I’ll cut off your most important bit. Got it?”

Savage triumph rose in her as Rodger nodded.

She spun on her heel and left him, moaning in pain as he slumped into his chair once more. Bastard deserved it. Perhaps her meaning wasn’t fully driven in. Maybe he could use another lesson...

A wave of nausea suddenly hit her. Val closed her eyes briefly, choking back vomit. She breathed deeply through her nose, focusing on moving through it. When she started to feel a little better, she straightened. She didn’t want to go back through the smoky front room, so she headed out the back.

When the door slammed open, Melanie jumped. She wore a robe over her sparkling body, and when she saw Val, her face went white. A phone was clutched in her hand and her mouth opened and closed as though begging for mercy. Val softly closed the door and turned to her.

"That Cunningham?"

Melanie flinched.

Answer enough. Val snatched the phone from her and snapped it in half. As the other feline shifter drew back, Val reached into her pocket and pulled out her wallet. She still had the money from a previous drop in it. Withdrawing the whole wad, she thrust it into Melanie's hands. Melanie's eyes widened as she stared at the money.

"Look." Val's kept her voice soft, a tone usually only her girls heard. "Get out of here. Away from this bastard. Away from this hellhole of a town. Get out before it's too late. Rodger likes curvy cats and I can promise he's got an eye on your... kitten." She stepped away, then turned back and smiled her most chilling smile. "Oh, and if you try to interfere with gang business again, I will mess you up. Friend or no friend of Ava's. Now give me your keys."

Melanie handed them over without a word.

***

Val sat on the hood of Melanie's clunker car at a rest stop three hours away from Coalfell. One arm wound tight around her waist while she held her phone to her ear. “Be a good girl for Auntie Ava and Uncle Jackson,” she told Freya, tears burning her eyes as the desire to hold her babies rushed over her. “I love you.”

“Love you too, Mama.”

She clamped her lip down hard on her teeth, fighting the urge to cry. Moments later, Jackson’s voice came over the line.

“They’ll be fine, Val. I promise.”

“I know. I don’t know when I’m going to be able to get back, though. I’m headed over to Ivywood. Lay low with Thunder for a bit.”

Jackson made a disgruntled noise. Typical big brother. It made Val smile, except it didn’t last long.

“Jackson...”

“Yeah?” Concern colored his voice.

Val lost her nerve. “Call me every night before putting the girls to bed, okay?”

“Sure.” Jackson chuckled. “I promise.”

She hung up without another word. Nausea washed over her again, but she knew that the pit toilets on offer here would only make it worse. Of all the dumb things—she had to go and get herself pregnant again, didn’t she? Worst timing ever.

Nothing to do about it now. She doubted that Cunningham would soften toward her just because she was preggers.

As she slid off the car's hood, a man strode from the trees. Tall, thin, pale. Smelling sweetly of rotten fruit. Val tensed. Sunset still hung in the west, making the vampire's fangs gleam red when he smiled. He was more muscular than vamps normally were. Smelled strange, too... almost meaty. Like a living thing.

"Valerie Masters?" he asked, as though he was greeting her on a runway. "Hello. My name is Cromwell. I'm the new king of the vampire clan near Coalfell."

Val rolled to the balls of her feet. "Right. So how come you're prancing around in daylight?"

Cromwell ignored her, his gaze sliding down her body. "I didn't know that the alpha's sister was so beautiful...

you'd make an excellent little pet, wouldn't you?"

"Fuck you!" Val sprang forward.

Before she could land a single blow, though, a dozen vampires suddenly burst from the trees. A ripple passed through her, warning her that she was crossing through into vampire territory. The hairs on the back of her neck prickled. Val hissed between her teeth, recognizing her mistake too late. She turned on her heel, intent on rushing back to the shifter side of the border.

Hands grabbed her arms and hair. They yanked her off her feet and dragged her into the forest. The road disappeared as she screamed and spat, twisting but unable to free herself. When they stopped, the vampires forced her to her knees before Cromwell. Val hissed, her heart hammering. The vampire smiled at her, clearly enjoying her struggles. She forced herself to still, just so he'd have something less to laugh about, and glared hatefully as he knelt in front of her.

"This is exactly what I needed. Thank you so much for delivering yourself right into my hands, Shadow. Your sacrifice will usher in a new chapter for vampire-shifter relations."

The vampires all around her guffawed with laughter. Cromwell grabbed her hair and yanked her head back, exposing her throat. His face took on a hideous hunger as he unhinged his jaws, ready to drain her dry.

# Chapter Four

*Blizzard*

Gabriel saw a vehicle parked in the rest area and turned off toward it. He had only a vague description of the car Val had stolen—Melanie seemed quite distracted when she was telling him about it—but that car seemed to fit.

What the hell was going on with her? Val was the last person he'd ever expect to act crazy like this and yet, here she was. Dealing drugs. Breaking wrists. Smashing phones. It wasn't like her at all. Was there trouble going on with the gang that he didn't know about? She had said that they were getting bored. Was the restlessness related to Jackson getting himself a mate? Did the gang see him as being weaker now?

Was Val having to prove that the Masters siblings were as tough as ever so that they didn't end up with a coup on their hands?

Gabriel wasn't sure what he'd do if that were the case. His involvement would just make things worse for Val and Tornado, but if the gang was getting ready for a civil war, it'd end up spilling over onto civilians. Something he could not allow.

Those thoughts were driven from his head as soon as he exited his car. Val's scent clung heavy to the area—along with the sickly scent of vampires.

The hair prickled on the back of his neck, and Gabriel immediately drew his gun. He crouched low between the cars, eyes scanning the area. His heart pounded against his chest. Val had been attacked by vampires again. Red sunlight still streamed in the sky; from the strength of the smell, they must have been here recently.

His teeth curled over his lips as he began to follow the trail. His ears strained for any noise in the forest, and, with luck, he picked up a bout of laughter. His stomach twisted sickeningly. His wolf pounded against his ribs, telling him to simply rush in and tear the vampires apart. But that would only lead to further trouble. So, he moved downwind before he entered the forest and slowly, methodically, so he wouldn't make a noise, began to creep up on the vampires.

What had Val gotten herself mixed up in this time? It would serve her right to get killed if she messed with vamps—as a shiver ran over him, indicating the charm placed on the border between shifter and vampire territory, he ground his teeth—especially messing with vamps on their own turf!

Soon, he could see them between the branches and bushes. He crouched low, observing. Val was held on her knees before an usually muscular vampire. He tensed when he caught the faint scent of blood.

The vampire grabbed her by the hair and yanked her head back. His fangs glittered in the dying light and Gabriel's wolf surged forward. He had shifted before he realized it. Just as he was about to leap forward, though, Val spoke, and the vampire froze.

"You kill me, you end up just like your former king," she spat, struggling against the vamps that held her down. "My brother will turn you into dust!"

A thrill of horror ran down Gabriel's spine. It was true. If Val was killed by vampires, there was nothing that would stop Tornado from hunting down and murdering every vampire he could, whether or not they were involved in her death. He wouldn't respect the treaty between them; vampires had every right to kill shifters that wandered onto their territory, that was why the warning was in place.

And Tornado, once he started killing, would be indiscriminate. He'd kill in vampire territory and the treaty would then demand that the vampires could pick a shifter at will, one for every one of their fallen comrades, and kill them.

“We’re counting on it,” the vampire laughed, yanking her head back again. “Oh, my sweet little leopard. Why do you think we chose you? The bond between you and your brother is strong. So strong that when you are dead, Coalfell will fall. Your brother’s place as alpha will weaken. He will be consumed with vengeance. It will be all too easy to provoke him into running a raid against my kingdom.”

Val didn’t respond, but she did stop struggling. So, she saw it too. Gabriel lowered himself to his belly and started inching forward, gaze sharp on the scene. As long as the vampire kept talking, he had a chance to get close enough...

“And then what?” Val’s voice shook; that drove Gabriel’s anxiety levels up. Adrenaline flooded his system.

"You provoke him into attacking you.... Because you want to have a war on your hands?"

The vampire laughed again, a triumphant gleam in his eye. The other vampires chuckled along with him. "Well, yes. But that's the long game, Shadow. No. Once Tornado is hellbent on killing every single vampire in existence, all I will need to do is invoke the Contract of Peace to get Typhoon to come and wipe the Coalfell chapter out. I have no intention of bowing before the shifters like other weak kings do. No. I will see my people rise once more."

"Aw, poor widdle vampire," Val taunted. "Your dung heap not good enough for you anymore?"

Her voice took on a familiar tone as Gabriel got himself into position. Now he just needed to wait for the right moment, so he could free her and they could get the hell out of vampire territory! The vampires that milled about the muscular one and Val were all eagerly watching the scene, the two that held her in place chuckling. Nobody expected help to arrive.

The vampire yanked her head back again. "Shifters. You think you are so clever. You live like animals. And now, you will die like one."

As he widened his jaws once more, Gabriel sprang in. He howled, drawing attention to himself, as he bowled into one of the vampires holding Val. His teeth locked around its arm, and he yanked it away from her before releasing it and lunging at the other. The vampire released Val to face him. The muscular vampire's cry of fury cut off to a howl of pain as Val head-butted him. Her claws swiped across his face.

Gabriel grinned and turned his attention back to his own vampires. Two of them came at him from either side and he lunged for a third and yanked it back in time for its two fellows to stab through its body with their long claws. As it shrieked, he flung the three of them to the side and leapt onto the back of another. Claws raked down his flank and he twisted, jaws snapping over the limb of his attacker. He wrenched his head to one side, pulling the arm clean off.

His wolf howled, driving for the kill, but he merely shouldered the maimed vampire aside and bit down into the thigh of another. He couldn't kill any of them. Not while in their territory.

From the corner of his eye, he saw Val lunging for the muscular vampire's throat. Her eyes were blood-red. Gabriel ripped away from the vampire he was fighting and threw himself over her. Her teeth grazed the vampire's throat but didn't find purchase. They tumbled together a few times, breaking clear of the ring of vamps. Val snarled, her spotted body twisting out from beneath him. She lunged again, and he clamped his teeth on her tail, yanking her back.

Fiery, burning pain erupted from his side. He howled, twisting away from the agony, to find a vampire pulling its fangs from his body. Everything seemed to stop as the green venom dripped from the vampire's mouth. It laughed.

Then Val screamed. His head whipped around to find Val stumbling away from the muscular one. Her blood shone red, mingled with the venom on the vampire's lips. Gabriel started moving toward her, but even as he did so, his head spun. His feet felt sluggish.

"This was most entertaining," the muscular vampire drawled. "But time is of the essence. Don't worry about your little girls, Shadow. They will be most useful in my plans."

Val's head whipped around. Her eyes were utterly blood-red now, no emotion on her face as her lips curled back into a snarl. A chill stole down his spine. She was in full berserker mode. There was nothing to stop her from killing these vampires. And for each life she took, another shifter would die.

As she lunged for the muscular vampire once more, Gabriel found himself again attacking her. This time he clamped his teeth over the back of her neck and dragged her several feet before she flipped onto her back and lashed out, her claws tearing across his belly. He howled with pain as she sprang back up and sunk her teeth into his shoulder.

"This is most amusing indeed," the vampire shouted, as the others laughed. "The cat and the dog, fighting each other."

Except now, Val's attention was solely focused on him. She had tasted his blood. To her, everything else will have disappeared. And so, he ran. A vampire sprang into his path to stop him, but he threw it aside and bolted through the trees. Behind him, Val's furious scream followed. Her claws caught the edge of his tail. His whole body throbbed with every step, but he didn't stop.

Sweet relief overcame him when he passed over the barrier line. It didn't last long, as Val sprang onto his back, tearing at his neck. He rolled, throwing her off. A few of the vampires charged after them, but at a shout from the muscular one, they retreated.

"They're dead anyway."

Well, that was true enough. Gabriel flattened his ears against his skull as he faced Val, her blood-red eyes not wavering. Blood pumped from various wounds, but she didn't seem to notice. Her claws were unsheathed, teeth bared. She leapt at him, a scream in her throat, and he dodged. She spun around and swiped at him. He dodged again.

He shot beneath his car, shifted to human form and opened the back door.

He threw himself in and slammed it shut as Val attacked. Her claws tore at the metal and she screamed again, biting the window.

How could he get her in here without locking himself in with her? He'd built his car to contain shifters he might have to pick up. If he could just get her in here, he'd be able to drive away. The vampires all gathered at the border, pointing and laughing. He snarled under his breath, wanting to tear off their heads.

He twisted, eye lighting on the seat belt.

Venom pounded through his body, leaving him shaking and full of the desire to kill.

He snarled once under his breath, then yanked the belt out and opened the door. Val threw herself in at once, tooth and claw bared and ready. As she began to savage him, he wrapped the belt tight around her neck and torso. As he tightened it, cutting off her breath, he slammed her into the seat and slid past her. When the door slammed shut behind him, she tore the belt right out of the seat and ripped it off before lunging at the back window.

The vampires howled in disappointment as he stumbled to the front and turned the car on. His hands shook. They charged. He stomped on the gas.

Within a second, they were gone.

***

Gabriel had had many friends who were bitten by vampires.

It always ended the same. The venom drove them crazy, made them rabid. Sometimes they killed others before they were put down, but they were always put down.

His head swam, visions of blood and anger burning in his mind. He couldn't even see the road before him anymore and when he came to a wide shoulder, he pulled off to one side. A glance in the back seat showed that Val had shifted back to her human form. Her hand pressed to her shoulder, where green venom bubbled between her fingers.

Gabriel reached for his gun, only to remember he'd dropped it in the forest. No matter. He leaned across to the glove compartment. Always kept an extra. As he began to load it, though, his door was suddenly yanked open. He looked up in time for Val to seize him by the neck and drag him from the car. Her hand caught his wrist, pinning the gun to the door, before she dropped to her knees. Her lips closed around the bite in his side and she began to suck.

By the way his body reacted, she might as well have been sucking on an altogether different part of him. His loins tightened, and he groaned, wrapping a fist in her hair. Heat sparked and spread throughout him. His wolf howled in delight. The gun slipped from his hand as he yanked himself out of her grasp. Both hands wrapped into her braids now, and he found himself thrusting his hips forward.

Val sat back. She spat out a mouthful of venom and sprang to her feet. Grabbing him by the shoulders, she turned him so that his body pinned her to the car. Her head tilted, offering her neck to his.

"Your turn." Her voice was husky and broken.

Gabriel stared at her, in utter confusion and shock.

"Suck out the venom!"

"But—that never works."

"It worked with Ava. Jackson was able to save her. Now do it!"

Gabriel's head dropped. The venom tasted like death, bitter, rotten. He sucked hard, spitting out mouthful after mouthful until it was just blood in his mouth. He pulled back then, staring down at the naked woman. His hands were on her hips, holding her in place, their bodies still pressed so firmly together that he could feel every movement Val made.

She looped an arm around his neck and ground her hips forward. Already hard, the movement was painful. His gaze dropped to her throat, wanting to kiss it. Wanting to take here, here and now. Wanting to make her scream his name before he ripped her throat out.

His wolf howled as he sprang away from her. He could feel it working to a frenzy. Val's attempts to suck out the venom hadn't worked. Any minute now, he was going to go rabid and kill her.

He lunged for the gun.

# Chapter Five

*Shadow*

Val didn't know if he intended to shoot her or himself. It didn't matter. That gun wasn't going to go off, not if she had a say about it. As Gabriel grasped the butt of the gun, she kneed him in the face. Gabriel grunted, stumbled back and lunged. She grabbed him by the throat and kicked his feet out from under him before seizing the gun herself.

The wolf froze.

"My God, Blizzard. Never thought you'd give up so easily."

She released the clip from the gun, letting the pack of bullets fall onto his chest. Their pelvis' pressed together. It would be so easy for her to shift position just a little bit and welcome him inside of her. Her leopard whined with need, wanting him more than she'd ever wanted anything before. But not like this. Val rolled off him and threw the empty gun onto the backseat of the car before she kicked that door shut.

"We need to get to a safe house."

"I'm going rabid, Val." His voice was tense. "I can't—"

"Don't be such a weakling. We get to the safe house, we lock ourselves in and let the venom pass." Her gaze traveled over his body. There were tattoos on his chest and down one side of his stomach that she hadn't known were there. She reached to touch them but pulled herself back.

Groaning in effort, she managed to pull herself to her feet. When she held her hand out to Gabriel, she got another good look at the length of his body. Including the very hard member jutting out from between his legs. She groaned at the sight of it; her leopard pawed at her, demanding she straddle him. It wanted to mate, now.

She closed her eyes as Gabriel took her hand and pulled himself up. Her mouth was dry as she shook her head.

"The venom," she grunted. "It awakens the animal brain. Going rabid isn't the right term. More like reacting to a situation where you feel cornered. Like the only option is to fight. But not just fight… Oh, God!" A tight ache twisted in her core as his heat brushed next to her. His hand found hers. Pressed her into the side of the car. Reluctantly, she opened her eyes to find his face inches from hers. “It also awakens... other animal instincts.”

“What do you mean?” Gabriel snarled.

“You know exactly what I mean!” She yanked a hand free and made to slap him, but he caught her and pressed her back again. “The need to mate. That primitive instinct... in you, it’s awakening your desire for dominance. To see me meek and submissive, for you to unleash all your desires on my body.”

Gabriel’s eyes screwed shut and he shook his head.

“In me,” Val panted, fighting the venom coursing through her body, “it’s telling me to claim a strong mate, a fierce protector for my children.”

His grip tightened painfully, and a snarl ripped from his throat. “I am not going to fuck you. I’m not doing this just because our heads aren’t screwed on right! I won’t!”

As if she was the one that was making him act this way.

“I won’t, either,” she spat back. “That’s why we need to get to the safe house. We can let the venom run its course there. We won’t have—”

Both of them moved at the same time. Mouths clashing in the middle, the woken hunger burning to a new pain. Val twisted her hands into his short hair, pulling him closer. Her body was on fire, the need for blood retreating as heat flared under her skin. Her body was too small, her skin too tight to contain it. Her clit throbbed with need.

She didn't know how she found the strength to pull away, but she did. She whimpered with the pain of separation even as she shoved against his chest, putting space between them. The two of them stood there panting, staring at each other. Finally, she pointed at the driver's seat.

"Get in."

Gabriel growled deep in his chest, making her insides squirm with desire again. Fortunately, he wasn't so far gone yet as to insist on her submission. Instead, he slid into the car. She climbed into the back, to put as much space between them as she could, and shut the door softly. They drove in pained silence, except for when Val directed him to the nearest safe house, a three-roomed cabin in the woods.

"It was designed for shifters who have been bitten," Val explained as they made their way inside. "The doors lock automatically from the inside and can only be opened with a specific series. One that the animal brain can't process."

"It's new," Gabriel grunted.

"Yup."

The two of them stared at each other, each before their respective doors. A thrill of fear ran down Val's spine as she opened hers. Even here, chances of survival were minimal, especially since they had no backup on the way. She opened her mouth, but what could she say? She closed it again and walked into the room.

***

The passing days were pure torture. Val's body moved from violently ill to trying to rip down the walls to masturbating furiously to vomiting all over the room. Dreams were fevered, equal parts ripping out Gabriel's throat and making love with him. When the worst of it retreated enough that she could figure out the lock to get out, she found Gabriel already waiting on the other side.

Two sleeping bags lay on the floor. Gabriel was in one, and Val zipped herself into the other without a word. She rolled over, pressing herself into Gabriel's side and his arm wrapped around her.

"I don't want to die," she whispered.

"What?"

"I can't leave my girls alone."

Gabriel's hand stroked her hair. It had become matted and frizzy during her imprisonment. He let out a sigh as he pulled her closer. "You aren't going to die. The worst of it is over, right? From here on, we'll just... get better."

"I'm a gangster. I fight vampires." Tears burned her eyes. "I'm going to die and leave them alone."

"You're a wonderful woman. Beautiful. Intelligent."

A warm feeling started to build in her chest. She pressed her face into him, breathing in that clean scent, and allowed herself to sleep.

***

Fevered dreams pressed in on her as she slept. Occasionally she woke and drank a little water, but mostly she just slept. Even in her dreams, she could sense Gabriel still with her. His firm, solid presence kept her from spiraling off into the darkness.

She wasn't certain how much time had passed before she woke drenched in sweat and knew the fever had broken. Gabriel lay beside her, also covered in sweat. Her whole body ached.

Val pulled away and climbed from the sleeping bag, stumbling a little, as she was still weak. The whole place stunk, but that was to be expected. She glanced around, orienting herself with the cabin. A sink sat on one side of the room, next to a toilet and a shower. A shower. With soap-on-a-rope hanging from the shower head. Relief washed over her as she stumbled for it.

It took several minutes for the water to run hot and by the time it had, the noise had woken Gabriel. He joined her under the stream of water, neither of them much caring about their nakedness as they helped one another clean themselves. Once she was satisfied with herself, Val took her sleeping bag outside, shook it out and then dumped it into the cold creek that ran just behind the cabin. She pinned it down with rocks, then went back inside. Gabriel threw his sleeping bag outside and rifled around in the cupboards. He withdrew two cans of beans and two more sleeping bags.

They ate, slept and, when she woke, Val felt much better. Stronger. She moved to the shower again, this time taking out her braid so she could wash her hair. She had cleaned herself before, but now she wanted to get a good scrubbing in.

Until Gabriel stepped up behind her. The heat of his body was stronger than the heat of the water as his hands slowly pressed against her shoulder blades. She expected them to slide down at once, but they sat there, warm and solid. Gabriel's face pressed into the back of her head. They stood like that, the warm water running over them both.

"What do you want?" Val asked, her skin tingling where his breath wafted across it.

"I don't know. You. Is this still the venom?"

Val leaned back against him, welcoming his embrace as his arms wrapped around her. "Do you still want to kill me?"

"No."

"Then it's not the venom."

She turned, her naked body pressed against his. The salt-and-pepper of his hair looked darker, pressed against his scalp and soaked with water. Lust shone from his eyes as he pulled her against him, but he hesitated, his mouth inches from hers. Waiting for permission? Val met his gaze, slowly closing the distance between them.

The heat that had been simmering under her skin flared back to life. Gabriel's kiss was fierce, determined. He suckled on her lower lip while backing her up against the wall, so the shower head sprayed down on both of them equally. He tasted of the beans they had eaten the previous night and she wanted more. Her arms wrapped around his neck, pulling him in tight against her. His hands moved from her hips to her back to her shoulders to her ass, as though he wanted to be touching her all over. Finally, he settled on holding her hip with one hand while reaching between her legs with the other.

She was already slick for him, the sexual tension from the past few days building to a peak. His thumb stroked her clit and a shiver ran through her whole body. Val arched herself to him, fighting to keep her footing on the slippery floor with one foot while she lifted her other leg to give him better access. His body undulated, brushing against her while he devoured her mouth.

Panting with desire, Val fumbled behind them and turned off the water altogether. Her clit was on fire as

Gabriel stroked it with firm, even pressure. Her eyes shut as her head fell back to the wall. He pressed against her belly, semi-erect and Val found him with her hand, stroking him with the same rhythm that he gave her. His dark eyes bored into hers.

He lifted her suddenly, pulling her away from the wall. Her legs circled his hips as he kissed her, walking blindly from the shower. When he set her down again, he turned her rapidly so her back was against his chest. One arm snaked around her waist, pulling her flush against him, while his free hand continued to toy with her clit. He ground into her ass as the fires flared throughout her body.

Need twisted inside of her, making her whimper, as his mouth delved into her neck. Shivers of pleasure left her trembling on edge and she clung to him. His kisses were becoming more urgent as he slowly laid her down, draping himself over her. The sleeping bags felt suddenly lumpy, but Val didn't care. Her whole body ached with need as she kissed every inch of Gabriel that she could reach. She spread her legs for him, reaching between their bodies to help guide him inside of her.

She didn't expect him to pull back, but he did. He panted as he wiped a drop of water from her cheek. "Is this okay?"

Something warm burst inside her chest. When was the last time she'd had a man ask her that question? She cupped his face in her hands and brought him down for another kiss. Their tongues tangled as he started to nudge in her. Then he pulled back once more, his expression a little harder than it had been before.

"I need a clear answer, Val. Is this okay?"

Val laughed softly, wrapping her fingers in his hair now. "Yes. Don't you think I'd let you know if it wasn't?"

Gabriel shrugged. "I guess I'd rather be certain than have you suddenly put me in a headlock. And you're good with me on top?"

It had been years since she had allowed a man to top her. Val hesitated a moment, warring with herself. She wanted to let him have his, yes. She wanted to be the receiver for once, rather than giving and giving and not getting anything back. But it was such a vulnerable position. With him on top of her, he could do anything he wanted and what could she do to stop him? Her fingers dug into his shoulders.

He must have seen the reluctance in her eyes, because he turned them both, letting her be on top. Her hair dripped into his face, but he smiled, tracing a hand over her back and then round to her breasts. "I like the view from down here anyway."

Val laughed, shaky. How could such a simple gesture be so disarming? The warmth in her chest, completely unrelated to the heat flaring under her skin, grew. She eased him inside of her, sighing with pleasure as he reached to every part of her, and began to grind against him. Gabriel groaned, his hands still exploring her body. His dark gaze smiled up at her as she leaned forward slightly, resting her hands against his chest.

His girth inside of her made everything feel that much tighter. She groaned in sweet agony, legs tense, spine erect. Her head fell forward as she ground hard against him. Pleasure sent shivering bolts up her spine and down her legs. His hips thrust up, matching her rhythm. His teeth clamped over his lower lip as he panted.

Her core tightened to a point where she couldn't take it anymore and bolts of electricity exploded through her. Her muscles turned to mush and she collapsed over her lover, writhing and whimpering and panting with desire that didn't seem to be anymore sated than when she started.

When they were both finished, her leopard curled up into a ball in her chest, yawned and settled down to sleep. Val rolled off Gabriel, panting for breath, as the shock waves still caressed her.

"Hey." His voice was breathy and hoarse as he touched her face. "What's wrong?"

It was only then that she realized she was crying. Val turned her face, not wanting to look at him. She sniffled, mortified by the tears still running down her face.

"Val?" He wrapped his arms around her. "What's wrong?"

"I'm pregnant."

## Chapter Six

*Blizzard*

His first thought was that there was no way she could know that fast.

Then it sunk in.

She was pregnant.

Val was pregnant. The woman he just had sex with was pregnant. His brain was slow on the uptake, due to the jelly-like sensation that still filled him. He licked his lips, wondering why she was telling him—so she couldn't pretend like he was the father in the future? So he wouldn't think he was and cause trouble? Because she was afraid? Because she had no-one else to tell?

A shudder ran through Val's body and he wrapped his arms around her, pulling her back against him. He kissed her shoulder, trying to show her everything was alright. "Hey. It's okay. You're going to be fine. Unless..." She had been bitten. "Are you afraid that the attack—"

"No." Val shook her head as she choked on a sob. "No, I'm not worried. I got bitten a few times when I was pregnant with Freya. I just..."

Gabriel waited a beat. "Who is the father?"

"I don't know."

Ah. He ran his hand down her arm. "Do you want him in the baby's life?"

Val snorted, a definite no for an answer. "They're all losers. I don't know what's wrong with me. I only sleep with losers."

Gabriel frowned. “I hope you’re not including me in that.”

“I am.” Val’s tone became petulant. “Only you’re worse. You’re a traitor, too.”

His wolf growled, and he withdrew his arms from around her. The warmth that had been budding in his chest evaporated at once. “Then why did you just have sex with me?”

Val shrugged, not looking at him. “Guess I was just desperately horny. Must have been the venom.”

The venom? No, it wasn’t that. Gabriel snarled as he launched himself to his feet. Were there any clothes in this place? It seemed stocked with everything else. He stomped away from Val as she remained lying there, naked and smelling of him. What was wrong with her? Why did she have to act like such a bitch? The venom. As if it hadn't worked its way out of their systems.

The door opened. Gabriel's head whipped around at the sweet vampire scent. He charged without stopping to look at the intruder; with a roar, he flung himself at him, only for the newcomer to clothesline him across the throat and bring him down. Gabriel coughed as he was pinned to the floor.

A familiar face peered down at him. Fangs flashed, and Gabriel called his wolf forward. Fur began to sprout along his body, but before he had a chance to fully transform, his attacker lunged for his throat. Gabriel threw an arm into its path. Teeth clamped down on his arm.

Great. I'm going to have to do this all over again.

He swiped at his attacker's face, claws ripping across flesh. Great drops of blood splattered over his face.

Wait. Blood?

His gaze finally focused as the attacker released his arm and wrapped his hands around Gabriel's throat. His mind whirled. Beneath the scent of vampire was the wild, musky smell of wolf—and the recognition clicked. This was Thunder, alpha of the Ivywood chapter of the Savage Brotherhood.

His fangs gleamed as he tightened his grip on Gabriel's throat and whatever relief had come with the realization disappeared at once. He bucked his body and punched Thunder in the kidneys, anything to break his grip. Thunder's eyes took on a maniacal gleam, and he began to slam Gabriel's head against the floor while choking him.

A snarl and a scream caused Thunder to look up. In the next second, Val's golden-yellow body rammed into him, knocking him off Gabriel. As the sheriff coughed and choked, Val threw Thunder to the floor and wrapped a paw around his neck before shifting back to human form. Or at least, partially. Fur still covered her body, fangs and claws sharp and deadly.

Thunder twisted his head to glare at Gabriel with so much hatred that he thought the alpha was going to throw Val off and come at him again.

"Don't even think of it," Val snarled. "He's with me, Thunder."

"I can smell that, Shadow. What the hell are you doing?"

Val snarled.

Thunder eased his head back, putting distance between her claws and his throat. "Let me up."

The leopard considered him for a moment before she eased off his back. Gabriel rolled to his knees, ready to defend himself if need be. Thunder didn't attack again, though. He sat, rubbed his throat and glared at Val. Gabriel's hackles rose and the desire to push her behind him made him start moving forward. He froze, though, as he remembered what she had said to him moments before.

"You'd better have a fucking good reason for bringing a traitor and a cop to a safe house in Ivywood territory,

Shadow. And it better not be because you wanted to fuck him without your brother finding out."

Gabriel was reminded that not all of the Brotherhood was on as good terms with him as the Coalfell chapter. He had no doubt, if Val wasn't here, he'd be dead in a second.

"Blizzard is instrumental in Coalfell for our work," Val replied, her voice cold, as though she wasn't the first to call him a traitor. "He keeps our boys out of jail and understands what we're doing. Don't even have to go through the mess of bribing him. 'Sides, he saved my life from a bunch of vamps and got bit for his troubles."

"So, you fucked him as a reward?" Thunder spat.

Gabriel rolled his eyes even as his muscles bunched. “Yeah, sure, whatever. We got info that Typhoon needs to—”

“Shut up or I’ll rip out your throat after all.”

Gabriel growled at him and Val stepped between them. She glared at Gabriel and he glared back.

“Yeah, we fucked,” she said, not looking at Thunder. “Because we were both bitten and that seemed like a better idea than tearing each other apart for the vampire’s amusement.”

She turned back to Thunder so that Gabriel couldn’t see her expression, but he could imagine that she had pulled a smug, superior look. His gut twisted. The vulnerability he had seen in her while they made love was utterly gone. Not that he blamed her. But it had started to fade the moment she called him a traitor. And he had an awful, sickening feeling that he was never going to see it again.

Thunder's gaze moved from Val to Gabriel and he jerked his head toward the door. "Get the hell out of here, Cop. And don't come back unless you want your head mounted on my wall."

"Very dramatic," Gabriel sneered, but got to his feet anyway. He didn't head for the door, though. Not when there was so much more going on here than he knew about. "I have as much right as anybody to know what the vampires are after. This new king's got a plan to get the Brotherhood fighting each other so he can wipe us out—"

"Us?" Thunder started forward and it was only Val punching him in the shoulder that stopped him. “You aren’t part of this, Blizzard. You left the Brotherhood. You turned your back on us. You don’t get to start demanding that you’re a part of this.”

Gabriel’s hands clenched. “Just because I’m against murder and drugs and other stuff that the Brotherhood has fallen into, doesn’t mean that I want vampires to run amuck. And yet here they are, running around in daylight, attacking prominent members of the Coalfell chapter. And what are you doing about it? Attacking me?”

Thunder started forward and once more Val pushed him back. She snarled, flashing her canines at him.

“For God’s sake!” She threw her hands into the air. “Gabe’s already naked, why don't you just pull it out to compare already?"

Thunder lifted a fist, whirling on her. Gabriel sprang forward before he could stop himself, pulling Val back. She turned on him, driving a fist into his stomach. As he hunched over, all the air escaped his lungs. As he wheezed, she pushed him toward the door, keeping her body between him and Thunder. The alpha, however, no longer looked as angry as he had been. No, now he looked positively amused.

"Get out of here, Cunningham. If there is anything you need to know, we'll tell you," Val spat at him.

Gabriel straightened, breathing shallowly to avoid hurting his lungs. He glared at her for a moment longer before he turned on his heel and marched out.

If she didn't want him there, fine. The Brotherhood had long since failed in their mission. His duty was to protect civilian lives, not the gang.

He had his own business to take care of. Fighting here, when he was still weakened, was insane.

He was just outside the door when a wave of nausea hit him like a freight train. His knees buckled. Behind him, he heard Val give a pained whimper. He turned to help her, but the world pitched, and everything went black.

***

He came to as he was being pulled out of his cruiser. A couple of men, shifters by the smell of them, gripped him around the arms and hauled him to his house. Everything spun around him, and he wondered if they had beaten him up. Then bile rose up his throat and he remembered. Vampires. But he'd gotten better. Had Thunder done something to him?

He lifted his head weakly and found that the two shifters now unlocking his front door were unfamiliar. His wolf growled, but that was about all it could do. With a groan, his chin fell back to his chest.

"Val," he mumbled.

"Shadow's being taken care of," one of the shifters spat. "Damn cop. Don't see why we don't just take his head."

The other snorted as they dropped him to the floor. "You heard Thunder. We're supposed to leave him here."

"He'd never know."

Gabriel tried to push himself to his hands and knees, but a foot pressed between his shoulder blades and pushed him back down. "You want to take on Thunder?"

The foot was removed and a flurry of footsteps told him the two had fled. Gabriel looked up, a tart insult on his tongue, but everything spun around again, and he laid his head down again. For a long time, he lay like that, not daring to move. Eventually, cool hands pressed against his hot body and he smelled the distinctive scent of cat.

He knew it couldn't be Val, but hers was the face that his mind put into place as the shifter lifted him from the floor and encouraged him to bed. Hers was the voice, panicked, that asked him what she needed to do. It was all Val, all around him, and he sank back into the darkness, holding her image in his mind.

***

The feline scent was still strong when he woke once more from a haze of fever and dreams. This time he felt like death. Every bit of him ached like he'd been in a fistfight and had come out on the bad end. Nails spiked through his brain and he screwed his eyes shut tight, wanting to sink back into the blissful unconsciousness. It wasn't going to happen, though.

He still smelled Val. His arm moved on its own, patting the bed beside him for her, even though he knew she wouldn't be there. That didn't stop the twist in his gut when he found the bed empty.

What had he been thinking? Why had he been so stupid as to sleep with Val? He should have had better control of his faculties. They didn't have any sort of relationship and this would just make the antagonism between them worse.

"You're awake." A female voice made him look up. Melanie stood in the bedroom door, looking torn between fury and relief. She marched in and the anger took over on her face. Her fists clenched, and she shook them at him. "You! You... dirty cop!"

Gabriel stared at her. "What are you doing here?"

"Taking care of you." Melanie huffed, still glaring at him. "Ava called me and told me to come over here and look after you. She said it was important that you didn't go to a hospital—and I know exactly why, too!"

So, they had told her about the vampires? It would make things a lot easier from here on out.

"I ought to call the FBI. Homeland security. The US marshals!"

Or not. Gabriel pushed himself up to a sitting position. His vision threatened to tilt, but he blinked hard and it stayed steady. He focused on Melanie again, who still glared at him as though he had mowed over her rosebushes.

"That would only make things worse. How would people react if they found out?"

"That their sheriff nearly died from an overdose? They'd be bloody furious, as they should be! No wonder you've let that gang keep pushing all their drugs. I thought you were in their pocket, but it turns out, you're in their hookah!"

What the hell was she going on about? Gabriel glared at her. He swung out of bed and opened his mouth to tell her that it had nothing to do with drugs, but stopped. He couldn't reveal the truth about vampires, especially not to someone like her, who'd most likely start blasting off about it on every social media platform out there.

"Not an overdose," he finally muttered.

Melanie snorted and rolled her eyes. "You had the exact symptoms that my coworker had. You can't tell me that it wasn't an overdose!"

"I was poisoned," Gabriel snapped and then stopped. His eyes widened as he understood what she had said. "Wait, you said that your coworker had those exact same symptoms?"

Melanie nodded, though she looked less furious now and a little more uncertain. Probably thinking about his declaration that he had been poisoned. He didn't care about that, though. He strode to her and seized her wrist, staring intently into her eyes.

"Tell me everything that happened."

## Chapter Seven

*Shadow*

There was an empty ache in the pit of her stomach when she woke and for a wild, fearful moment, Val thought it meant she had lost the baby. When she closed her eyes and concentrated, though, she could hear its heartbeat, rapid and fluttering, like hummingbird wings, and she let out a sigh of relief.

So then why this ache?

She peeled her eyes open, which was difficult given the state she was in now, and found that she was lying in a huge bed. Seriously it was bigger than a king. A frown crossed her face as she started to sit up, only to find herself utterly naked. What had happened here? She remembered going to the safe house with Gabriel and the hazy fevered dreams there... then making love... Thunder had shown up and everything after that was a blur.

Speaking of Gabriel... she turned to the empty side of the bed and glared at it. Why was she alone in this giant bed? Where had he run off to? Not that it mattered. She knew what he was like, he was a love 'em and leave 'em kind of lover, just like her.

The ache in her stomach increased.

Val shook herself off and climbed out of bed. Some clothes were folded over a chair nearby and she threw them on. They were slightly too tight, but only just. Once she was dressed, she took a moment to assess herself. She ached, but only in that 'I've been sick' sort of way. There was a faint smell of wolf in the room, but the only scents clinging to her skin were Gabriel's and her own.

Good. Thunder might be part of the gang and an alpha, but she didn't know him enough to trust him not to try anything while she was unconscious. It seemed like he hadn't, though, so she didn't have to kill him.

She headed out, still feeling shaky, but that was because she had been unconscious for... it had to be at least a week. It took that long for vampire venom to run its course. Probably longer than that, even, since she was pregnant and her immune system wouldn't be fully up to snuff.

As she stepped out of the bedroom into a lavishly decorated hallway, she spotted Thunder coming toward her, carrying a tray of food. He grinned when he saw her and even had the audacity to wink.

"Morning, Sleeping Beauty. I wasn't sure when you were going to wake up. Don't tell me that the infamous Shadow can't hold her vamp venom."

Val grunted at him and grabbed a slice of toast off the tray. It was slightly overdone, but she didn't care as she gobbled it up.

"Where am I?" she demanded, glaring at him. "Why'd you move me?"

"You compromised the safe house with that cop." Thunder's face twisted in disgust. "So, I brought you to Hurricane's place."

Val choked on her toast. "*Hurricane*?" she spat furiously.

Considering how hostile he was towards Gabriel, this was the last thing she had expected. Gabe might have turned cop, but he still helped them out when called upon to do so. But *Hurricane*? Her lip rose in a sneer as she eyed the food tray contemptuously. That was food bought by blood money.

"So, you're all murderous toward Blizzard, but you still like to hang out here with this traitor?"

Thunder growled at her. "Watch it. You are my guest in Ivywood. I'm not above throwing you out. Or letting Typhoon know about your... indiscretions."

Val frowned for a moment, then recalled a missing piece of memory. Thunder trying to kill Gabriel, her interfering. So, this was more than about her sleeping with him. A knot twisted in the center of her empty stomach. She had said something to Gabriel, hadn't she? Something that had made him angry… what was it?

She shrugged, aware that Thunder was still staring intently at her. "I have my reasons."

"And those are?"

"Coalfell's affairs are none of yours."

Thunder snarled, moving closer as though he intended to intimidate her into talking.

*Puh-lease.*

"That doesn't explain why you brought me to a traitor's house, Thunder."

"He—"

“Is as much a traitor as Blizzard.”

“Hurricane never tried to kill an alpha. Any comparison between him and your cop ‘friend’ will only get you into trouble here, Shadow.”

The chapters often worked together on important issues. Ivywood, being the closest to Coalfell, was very important to them. They worked with Thunder often when things cropped up. Starting any sort of bad blood here could potentially end in disaster for them. Didn’t Cromwell want to have the Brotherhood wipe themselves out for him?

But she hated to back down. There was nothing more she could say about Hurricane without starting problems, though, so she took a different route.

"You had better have kept your hands to yourself while I was sleeping."

Thunder rose his lip in a sneer. "Why would I want to touch *you*? You're a surly, unfeminine, foul-mouthed woman. Besides, I don't like cats."

"Ah, no pussies for you?" She couldn't stop herself as she laughed. "I didn't know you were a dick man."

The tray came at her. Val swiped it away as coffee splattered against the wall. Even as she started moving to defend herself, Thunder had rammed into her. He used his weight to throw her against the wall and pinned an arm over her throat. Not hard enough to cut off her breathing, but enough to hurt. Fury radiated off him as he snarled again.

"Homophobic 'jokes' like that are a really good way to get on my bad side, Shadow. Don't forget that I know all the good places to hide bodies."

Val glared back at him, ready to claw his eyes out, but then she remembered. Thunder's little brother was gay. And he'd been beaten to death because of it. The fight went out of her at once. If her brother had suffered that, or one of her daughters?

"Sorry," she muttered. "I didn't mean it that way."

Thunder released her. "Doesn't matter if you meant it. It was still like that."

"Ahem."

Val glanced over to find an unfamiliar woman staring at the two of them. She wore a slinky red dress, her brown hair done in perfect curls and her face expertly contoured. Strappy heels finished off the ensemble and Val had to wonder what sort of life a woman like that would live, that she never found herself having to fight. She herself could never dare to wear heels. What if she was attacked? She had to fight at a moment's notice.

"Hello." The woman sashayed forward, glared at the mess on the floor, then smiled up at Val. "My name's Roxanne. Or Roxy, whatever you prefer. Now that you're awake, I assume you'll be leaving?"

Thunder growled. "She's not going anywhere."

Roxy sent him a look of pure malice. “And you’re going to keep her a prisoner, are you?”

Thunder glared right back.

With a snort, Roxy turned back to Val. “Sorry that I don’t have anything of yours to give you. This one,” she jerked her thumb at Thunder, “brought you round stark naked. But you don’t have to worry, I kept a close eye to make sure nothing happened.”

Val nodded stiffly at her, while Thunder’s growls reached a new pitch.

“I am not a *rapist.*” From the look in his eye, he was imagining tearing out Roxy’s throat right now.

“He’s not,” Val assured her.

“You’re a feline, but you smell like wolf.”

"I have many lovers who are wolves." Val stepped around Thunder. She nodded at Roxy. "Thanks for your help. I'll need to borrow a bike."

Thunder grabbed her arm. "You're not going anywhere until I have some answers."

Before Val could slap him off her, Roxy had come to her rescue. She seized Thunder's wrist and yanked his arm around his back before slamming him into the wall. Her teeth bared, and a low, threatening growl emitted from her throat. Thunder snarled and started to push himself back, but Roxy leaned her towering weight against him. Impressive for a woman wearing six-inch heels.

Val smirked and was about to thank her (while assuring her she didn't need help) when the smile dropped from her face. There, plain as day on Roxy's shoulder, was a tattooed lily. Her stomach dropped. That lily was used by a local prostitute ring.

She snarled low in her throat and Roxy glanced back at her. Seeing her eyes locked on the tattoo, Roxy released Thunder and turned her back, now looking warily at Val.

Val shot Thunder a hateful look, then focused on Roxy again. "Are you here by your own free will?"

Roxy narrowed her eyes for a moment, then nodded stiffly. "Yeah. You don't have to worry about me."

"Okay." Val relaxed. "Good. Cause I'd hate to have to ruin these carpets by killing Thunder for getting into trafficking."

“She’s not mine,” Thunder said sulkily as Roxy released him. He shoved a finger in her face. “And you, you’re not in Brotherhood business, so just butt out of it.”

Roxy shrugged. “Whatever. You big boys with your big bikes.”

She rolled her eyes as she walked away, and Val smirked after her. She liked Roxy. The smirk quickly dropped when she focused on Thunder again. Clearly being pinned had done nothing to improve his mood. He folded his arms and glared at her.

“Typhoon wants answers. What the hell did you do to provoke the vampires?”

“I didn’t *do* anything.”

From the floor below, a deep, rich, authoritative voice spoke. "That isn't what they're saying."

Her blood ran cold as she looked over the banister to find Typhoon staring up at her. He was a huge wolf, bigger than any she had ever known, including her father, who himself had been monstrous. There was a reason why he was the alpha over all the Brotherhood. Why he never had a need for an enforcer himself.

Coalfell had been in hot water ever since Ava. It wouldn't take much for him to believe whatever lies Cromwell was telling him about her.

A fire lit in her chest when she saw the vampire standing right beside the alpha. She snarled under her breath. How much trouble would she get in if she ripped the ugly bastard's throat out, here and now? But while the vampire looked pleased, almost gleeful, Typhoon looked seriously pissed off. Thunder started down the stairs, stopping to arch his brow at her.

Val followed, hands clenched. So, she was going to be slandered to her face, it seemed. If this was going to go the way she expected it, she might just tear out Cromwell's throat before it was over.

Typhoon turned on his heel and walked away. As Val followed him, she saw Hurricane hurrying up the stairs. She sneered at him. *That's right, Coward. We all know what you're like with vampires.*

Once they were in a parlor—once again, decorated with useless things like an empty bowl that probably cost more than her whole house—Typhoon turned to her and folded his thick arms. His glare was like a firebolt, but she wasn't about to let herself be intimidated.

"He and his cronies attacked me in Shifter territory, then dragged me over to vamp territory to kill me," she snarled, glaring at Cromwell. "With the express purpose of destabilizing the Coalfell chapter and to turn the Brotherhood against each other so they could wipe us out."

Typhoon frowned. "And you know this how?"

"'Cause he went on about it like an idiot."

Cromwell frowned at her. "She came into our territory, spying on us. Stirring up trouble. I demand that she be handed over to the vampires at once, for proper measure to be taken."

"Once I have proof of your claims, I will." Typhoon turned to the new king and glared at him now. Val couldn't help but feel relief that it was no longer directed at her. Typhoon continued. "I'm not about to start handing over pregnant women to the slaughter."

He knew? Panic started to well inside of her, and she froze when Cromwell turned delighted eyes on her. Something almost maniacal gleamed in his eye as a smile spread across his face.

"Pregnant? Well, then, this changes... everything." Even before he pulled the old, yellowed scroll from the inside of his suit jacket, Val knew everything was going to hell. Once she saw the scroll, though, her gasp died in her throat.

"The Contract of Peace!"

Cromwell waved it about and laughed. "Yes, little kitten, this is the contract of peace. The document that has held you animals in line long enough for my people to rebuild our numbers. The old kings may have forgotten why it was we allowed ourselves to be subjected to ink and paper for so long, but I have not."

He reached into his pocket and withdrew a lighter. Val gasped and started forward. Typhoon grabbed her arm and yanked her back, then did the same with Thunder. His expression was grim as Cromwell flicked on the lighter and lit the edge of the contract. Val's heart pounded, the smell of smoke thick around them.

When the contract was nothing but ash, Cromwell smiled up at them. “We will no longer be trod on by your filthy kind. A new age is about to start. And your child…” His gaze lit on her belly and a loud, malicious laugh bubbled from his throat. “Or should I say, your *children*, will help us usher it in.”

Val lunged forward. She didn’t stop to think; nobody threatened her girls! A howl of fury burst from her, but before she could land a single punch, Cromwell shot into the air. He hovered there, still cackling, then sped out a window. The shard rained down on them. Typhoon seized Val’s wrist and yanked her aside, and she whirled on him. She lifted a fist, ready to attack, but the look in his eye stopped her.

Fury, worse than anything she'd ever seen before, shone from his eyes.

"Thunder, get Shadow back to Coalfell safely." He glowered at the broken window. "I thought that this might happen... Cromwell's a fool, though. Thinks he's five steps ahead of us. Well..." A grin crossed his face. "We'll see about that."

# Chapter Eight

*Blizzard*

Hospitals always weirded Gabriel out. They were loud, smelly and yet, at the same time, so very quiet and clean. He had to put aside his discomfort, though, in order to get to the bottom of this. By this time, the people who had 'overdosed' on drugs should have shown marked signs of improvement. Even already been released from the hospital.

When he asked the doctors, they had no explanation for it. When he inspected the patients himself, what he found only confirmed his worst suspicions. The shifters who had overdosed were showing signs of rabidity. The humans were showing signs of becoming vampires.

So, the drugs were tainted after all. But not with the usual stuff, with vampire venom.

Once he was finished with the hospital, Gabriel called Melanie to the station so he could find out more. He sent Katie to locate Tornado, to tell him about what they had discovered. Maybe that would inspire the Brotherhood to start sharing information back to him.

Melanie arrived looking exhausted and upset. Gabriel offered her coffee, which she declined, then perched on the edge of her chair while she waited for him to talk. He didn't know if she still believed he was a drug user, but that was hardly relevant anymore. Right now, she was his only informant. He just hoped the gang hadn't gotten to her yet. Val knew it was Melanie, but she had also been very busy lately.

A pang hit his stomach as he thought about Val and her revealed pregnancy, but tried to put it from his mind. Right now, he had other things to concentrate on.

"Do you know where your friend got her drugs from?"

Melanie's lips pressed tight together.

"I can't help you if you don't tell me. I believe that the same person responsible for dealing the tainted drugs also poisoned me."

Her shoulders sagged. "My boss. At the... at the club. He likes to give his favorite girls something as a bonus... at least, that's what he says. Really, it's to keep them hooked and keep them coming back. There's a lot of shady things that happen there," Melanie added, looking up. "But it's the best paying gig in the town. How else am I supposed to get enough money to leave this place?"

Gabriel sighed. He knew all too well that Coalfell had a way of sucking people in and trapping them. Melanie wasn't the first woman to turn to such desperate measures to try to fight her way free, nor would she be the last.

He paused a moment, considering her. She was a beautiful woman. Her curves were bounteous, all her proportions just right. With her strong sense of right and wrong and her willingness to put herself on the line for others, she was exactly the type of woman that he ought to be lusting after. The kind of woman he should want. The forever sort of woman, the one that would be a perfect mate.

And instead, he kept thinking of Val. This had been going on for longer than he knew. It was the realization of feelings that had slowly crept up on him, not the feelings themselves. Even though it made no sense. They were terrible for each other. He was a cop, she was a gangster. She was a single mom, he had never thought much of having kids. Not to mention the age difference, although that honestly didn't bother him much—Val wasn't the kind who did anything she didn't want to do. Still, it was another reason why the two of them weren't meant for one another.

So why did he feel so protective of her, then?

Gabriel chugged the rest of his coffee and sat. Rather than making him feel more energized, he felt more tired than ever. For a moment he rested his face in his hands, breathing deeply and trying to clear his mind. This business with the vampires and the gang and Val was too much. Maybe he was just getting too old for it all.

"Sheriff?"

*Concentrate, Blizzard.* He paused for a moment, surprised at calling himself his old nickname, then shook it off. He looked back up at Melanie and nodded grimly. "Thank you for your help, Miss Seymore. I think it would be best if you kept your distance from the club and any other dirty business for a while. If you need help getting out of town, I'll be more than happy to put you into contact with people who can give you some aid."

Melanie nodded, then frowned. She fidgeted, pulled the sleeve of her sweater over her hand and twisted the cuff. "Sheriff... I'm afraid for Ava and Lily. You know them?"

"Of course. What are you afraid of?"

"I'm afraid they're going to get hurt. It seems like Jackson Masters loves them, but he's a gang member. Into all sorts of shady shit. And even if he doesn't eventually hurt them, what's to stop rival gangs from going after them? Not to mention his psychopath sister!"

"Jackson very nearly lost his position in the gang, even his life, for Ava. He would never hurt her and if you think that he'd hurt his daughter, then you don't know anything about wolves. We are very protective of our families." Gabriel leaned forward, frowning still.

"And if you think that Val would ever hurt them..."

"She broke Rodger's wrist and smashed my phone!"

Gabriel rolled his eyes. "From what I've heard, Rodger deserved more than a broken wrist. Especially since he gets girls hooked on drugs so he can make them do what he wants," he added when Melanie opened her mouth. "Val is fierce. She's a foul-mouthed, violent woman, but only when she has to be. She protects what is hers. Ava became hers as soon as Jackson fell in love. Lily is hers just as much as her own daughters."

Melanie gasped softly. "She has kids?"

If Val was here, she'd probably snap his neck for revealing such a thing.

Luckily for him, she wasn't here. "Yeah. They're her life."

"How do you know all this?"

Gabriel ran his hand through his salt-and-pepper hair. "Because I was once part of the Savage Brotherhood. Left to join the military and when I came back, I decided to be a cop. Painted a big target on my back. But I know how these things go, and I know that if it wasn't Jackson and the Brotherhood here, it'd be someone else. If they don't pass out their drugs, someone else will get in with dirty drugs. Sometimes you have to dance with the devil if you want to save lives, Melanie. Nothing is ever as clear-cut as it seems."

The feline shifter shrank back from him. Her eyes were huge in her skull, her chest heaving. Sweat beaded her forehead and he could see the flight instinct starting to kick in. She looked just like a feral cat cornered by a wolf, knowing that its end was near. Gabriel put his hands in his lap and stayed very still, so as not to frighten her more.

"I'm not going to hurt you," he said gently. "I'm just trying to help you understand. The gang does do terrible things. But there are always worse people out there. Jackson doesn't allow things like sex trafficking. They're determined to clean up the streets when it comes to the tainted stuff that put your friend's life in danger."

Melanie eyed him doubtfully, still wound up. "So, what you're saying is that they're the good guys in this situation?"

Gabriel barked out a laugh. “Good guys? No. I would never say that. Because there are no good guys. Not here, not in towns where gangs don’t exist, not anywhere. No matter where you look, you won’t find the perfect heroes that exist in stories and movies. They’re not as bad as some people out there, but that doesn’t mean they’re good. Hell... doesn’t mean *I’m* good. Now, you’re Ava’s friend. That gives you some immunity. That doesn’t mean they won’t come after you. Stay clear of the Brotherhood, Miss Seymore. Get out of Coalfell as soon as you can.”

He could see that she thought it was a threat, but didn’t bother correcting her. It might as well be a threat. If she didn’t get out, she was going to get herself hurt, or worse. There were plenty of people outside the gang who wouldn't like her interference.

Once she was gone, Gabriel grabbed his hat and his keys. There was still investigating to be done.

***

The bar looked even more rundown than it had been last time he'd been in here. Gabriel couldn't stop himself from smirking as a rush of memories came over him once he was in the dim, smoky interior. He had spent many nights here, getting drunk after a successful job. Getting drunk, having sex and waking up the next morning with a splitting headache and utterly naked in the alley behind the bar.

Everybody stopped when he entered. Drinks halfway to mouths, cigarettes hanging from fingers. It was expected. This was gang territory. Nobody came in here unless they were looking for trouble.

Gabriel marched up to the bar, ignoring the looks he got, and focused on the bartender. "Les."

The older wolf eyed him skeptically. "Blizzard."

"Just Cunningham now, if you don't mind." Gabriel kept his voice low and even. Non-threatening. "Tornado's not answering his phone and I need some information."

Les shook his head. "You should know better than to start poking around here, Bliz—Cunningham. Most of the folks here would like to see you in the ground."

Gabriel smiled without humor. “Perhaps an exchange of information, then? There’s been a third party pushing drugs into Coalfell. Not the Brotherhood. I know because Val told me. These guys—”

“I’m sure I know nothing about that.” Les scrubbed furiously at a clean spot on the bar. “Go home, Blizzard. We’ll take care of our own business.”

There was a time when the gang was family to him. Gabriel took a seat, knowing it was dangerous, but also knowing that this was his best bet for getting hold of Jackson. Katie hadn’t been able to find him and with the alpha not picking up his calls, a more direct approach was needed.

The door to the bar opened and a familiar scent wafted in. The overly sweet scent that had accompanied the victims of the new drugs in the hospital. Gabriel turned on his seat to see Eric and Basil, two newcomers to the gang, strut in. Their eyes were glassy and by the way they walked, he could tell they were high. He tensed. If they'd taken the stuff tainted with vampire venom...

"Look!" Basil shouted, louder than was necessary. He laughed as he pointed at Gabriel. "It's the cop!"

"I am a cop," he agreed. "And whatever you're high on has vampire venom in it."

The hostile looks that were still being thrown his way turned to alarm. Eric and Basil looked shocked for a minute. They glanced at each other and then started to laugh weakly. They stumbled to the bar, parting to sit on either side of him. Eric slammed his fist against the bar twice, while his face started to turn a nasty shade of green.

"Ridiculous," Basil grunted. "Vampire venom? You're just trying to get us to admit that we're high."

"Which we're not," Eric added quickly. "No drugs on us!"

His eyes rolled into the back of his head and he slumped against the bar. Gabriel caught him quickly and lowered him to the floor, just in time to catch Basil as he passed out. He checked their pulses to find their hearts beating fast and erratic. Bits of foam gathered at the corners of Basil's mouth, while Eric started to seize.

Throughout the bar, people started to call out in worry. Gabriel quickly rolled the two of them to their sides, just as they started to vomit. Both of them were green by this time.

"Dammit, you kids!" Gabriel let out a stream of curses. "Don't you recognize the smell of vampires anymore?"

He patted down their pockets and found a small bag of white powder. All it took was one taste to know that it was tainted. With a growl, he glanced up. The gang stared at him, frozen. He straightened, moving to one side for Les to take care of Eric and Basil.

"You, call an ambulance to get these idiots to the hospital," Gabriel ordered. "The rest of you, do a call out and get people to bring in the drugs that this other gang is selling. Bring the dealers to the alphas."

There were a couple of nods and some of them started for the door before they froze again. The rest of them glanced at each other, caught somewhere between nervous and confused. Gabriel opened his mouth to repeat himself when Les coughed. He glanced down in annoyance to find the bartender looking at him with a wry look on his face.

"You're not a member anymore, Blizzard."

Right. It had just been so easy, falling back into that role. For the people who had moved to obey him, too. But he wasn't part of the gang. They had no reason to obey him.

The door opened again, bringing with it a feline scent. Gabriel whirled toward the door to see Val and Thunder stalk into the bar. They froze as they took in the scene. Val's eyes widened while Thunder's narrowed. For a moment, they all stood there, tension enough to strangle the words from his throat.

Even so, relief rose in him. Val looked a little tired, but overall, fine. She was okay.

His relief was short-lived, however, when she grunted at him and sneered. "What are you doing here, cop?"

He opened his mouth furiously, about to ask was she really going to treat him like that after they'd had sex, but stopped again. This was certainly not the place. He'd end up a laughing stock and she'd be hard-pressed to justify her actions. Still, he didn't like the way she sneered at him. Behind her, Thunder smirked.

"I have reason to believe that Cromwell's the one pushing drugs into Coalfell," he replied, keeping his expression stony. "These two idiots took some of that stuff and are suffering from vampire poisoning."

Val frowned. She hurried over and checked over Eric and Basil herself. They had both stilled and were panting, sweat dripping from their faces. She let out a stream of curses as he had done and got back to her feet.

"Call 911 and get these bozos to the hospital," she ordered. "Mark, Alan, I want you to track down the people that are selling the tainted drugs. The rest of you, get out there and find me everybody who's bought any. Bring any dealers you find back here to be questioned by the alpha. Get going!"

A flurry of activity answered her orders. Val turned back to Eric and Basil, worry pinching her face.

"So, they found a way to turn people without biting them," she mumbled. "Or at least... to weaken us. Les, call Jackson. Get him down here."

Thunder glared at Gabriel for a moment before he headed into the back. Val took a step after him, then stopped and looked at Gabriel. A wry grin crossed her face and she waved her hand for him to join them.

"Better come along, Blizzard. We've got grim news that will affect you, too."

# Chapter Nine

*Shadow*

Thunder glared his protests at her, but she ignored him. This wasn't his turf. This was Coalfell and next to Jackson, she held the top rank. If she wanted Gabriel to sit in on this discussion, he would. He needed to know what was going on in the town. Jackson kept him in the dark when it was just gang business, but this was about vampires.

Her stomach twisted as she led the way to the backroom, trying to ignore the unease that Gabriel's presence brought. It wouldn't be so bad if it was just hatred or anger, as it usually was. No. This time her cheeks had to flush and her heart beat faster. Traitorous body! She preferred it when she was throwing up all over the place.

It would be much better to feel sick than to keep thinking about the way his breath felt against her skin. The sparks that ran up her thigh as his fingers caressed it. The way her core flared to life when his naked body pressed against hers. The soft grunts he made as she ground against him, the look in his eyes as his hands caressed her.

A shiver ran down her spine as he brushed past her and shot her a furious look. She had said something... what was it?

Well, it hardly mattered.

Val cleared her throat as she sat down, avoiding looking at Gabriel. They had done what they had done and, clearly, she hadn't been in her full faculties, otherwise she'd remember what she had said to make him angry. So, it was best if she just forgot it ever happened and returned to how she felt toward him before. Angry, betrayed, wanting to tear his throat out every time she saw him. It would be so much better than trying to sort out the mess of emotion she found herself in.

Although, if it had just been vampire venom which caused her to sleep with him, why did she want him so bad now?

His presence was like a lightning rod and her body pure energy. Even as she tried to ignore him, she could feel herself being pulled back to him, again and again. Her leopard beat its paws against her chest, wanting to go to him, to curl around his body and playfully nip at his neck. It wanted her to lay down here and now, presenting herself to him and receive the fullness of what he could give her.

Thunder was glaring at her now and she glared back.

"Have something you want to say?" she demanded.

He snorted and looked away.

Val glanced at Gabriel. There was a reason she wasn't talking, wasn't there? It was because she wanted to wait for Jackson to arrive, so she wouldn't have to explain multiple times what was going on. It wasn't because she was suddenly tongue-tied, sitting this close to a man she wanted, but shouldn't. Thunder would be a much better choice. At least they weren't on opposite sides...

Thunder wouldn't make a good dad for her girls, though.

Her hands clenched, and she turned her face away. How had Typhoon known she was pregnant? Was it Roxy who had told him? She hadn't told anybody—well, except for Gabriel. He didn't really count. She was just telling him so that things didn't get weird when she started to show. She didn't want him claiming her kid as his... and he wasn't the sort of guy who would take on the responsibility of being a dad to four children who weren't his.

Was that what her leopard wanted? To have a mate who could help her protect her babies?

"Val, are you gonna tell me what's going on or not?"

She shoved all thoughts of romance and mates from her mind as she turned to Gabriel. He was tense, jaw tight and eyes blazing. She couldn't help but notice that he was very carefully not looking at Thunder. The tension between the two of them was thick enough to pluck from the air and weave a basket. Gabriel rose a brow at her and she leaned back in her seat.

"I'm waiting for Jackson. Better say everything only once. It's more efficient that way, isn't it?"

Gabriel narrowed his eyes at her.

"For God's sake." Thunder's voice was almost sulky as he rumbled. "If you two are going to start trying to Romeo and Juliet this shit—"

"They died, genius," Gabriel interrupted. "Only an idiot would want to follow in their footsteps."

Thunder rolled his eyes. "What were you doing here anyway? Isn't this place firmly the Brotherhood's territory? Were you planning on getting shot... or maybe you were looking for your lady love?"

"Call me that again and I'll rip out your throat," Val hissed.

Thunder opened his mouth, but seemed to think better of it.

"I found out that the drugs that Val's been combating are laced with vamp venom. There are all kinds of people in the hospital showing signs of it. It seems to just wipe out the shifters, give them a small dose, but not enough to cause full rabidity. The humans, though... I can't really tell, but they might be on their way to becoming full vampires. And we still don't have an answer for how Cromwell can stroll around in daylight."

Val drummed her fingers against the armrest. Eric and Basil had gone and gotten drugs from a slimy secondary source. Once they pulled through this, they'd have to suffer the consequences of their actions. Of more immediate concern was the humans who'd taken the drugs. The last thing they needed was a hospital to suddenly become a breeding ground for new vamps.

"We'll have to kill them." Thunder seemed to read her mind. He shook his head, face grim as Gabriel tensed.

Val nodded. "I'll get together a team. We'll figure something out... This isn't going to be pretty. I'll have to get volunteers who are willing to get life sentences in jail if it comes to that. Gabriel, you can—"

"No."

She turned to him, eyes questioning.

"If we can survive the venom without going rabid, then there has to be a way to stop the humans from turning into vampires."

Had he gone soft? Val sucked on her teeth, fighting an irrational surge of anger. "How do you plan to do that? Are you going to fuck them all into being human again?"

Gabriel's eyes blazed. "If that's what it takes, I'll do it! I've killed too many good people because they were bitten and now that I know there's another way, I can't just go back to wholesale murder!"

Her heart nearly seized at the raw emotion in his words. Because she knew exactly what he meant.

Before her parents were murdered, Gabriel was their enforcer. He was to them what she was to Jackson. Their greatest support, the one who did things nobody else would. When she had become Jackson's enforcer, she'd had to kill people, too. Friends who had gotten bitten and lost their minds, who would have killed her and others if they had gotten the chance.

If she had figured out a little earlier that it didn't have to end that way...

She leaned back in her chair, suddenly exhausted. It was so hard, living like this. Sure, there was excitement and fun, but there was also so much violence and death. How much more of it could she take? She wanted to be part of the gang so she could save lives from vampires. How many had she managed to save? And how many more had she killed?

Even as regrets started to rise up in her, she battled them down with pure fury. What made Gabriel think that he was so much more special than the rest of them, that he got to say what happened?

"Guess fucking is all you're good for," she spat at him, then smiled. "That, or betraying people who trust you."

For a moment, she thought he was going to attack her. She wanted him to attack her. Then she could put aside all these feelings that had started to develop. If he laid so much as a finger on her, she could go back to hating him and leave it there.

He didn't attack, though. His muscles bunched, and his lips curled back to reveal a snarl, but he didn't so much as move. "Say whatever you want, Valarie. But when the guilt of all your dead starts to snap you in half, don't expect any sympathy from me—or any fucking."

Val pressed her lips together. If Thunder wasn't here... but it was a good thing he was. It stopped her from pouring out her heart like a broken schoolgirl.

"Your parents never wanted you to be part of the gang. Did you know that?" He leaned forward, eyes blazing. "I knew I needed to get out before this life chewed me up and turned me into a hard, bitter killer... Can you say that it's not too late for you? Would your daughters be proud of the person their mother is?"

Val leaped to her feet, a hiss on her lips.

Thunder lunged. He grabbed Gabriel by the collar and all but threw him toward the door. "You're finished here. Whatever Tornado wants you to know, he'll let you know."

Gabriel snorted. He glared at her for a moment longer, as though expecting her to say something. When she didn't, he turned on his heel and left the backroom. He slammed the door on the way out. Val's knees suddenly became shaky and she sat, hard, while clutching her head in her hands.

"You okay?" Thunder's voice was oddly soothing.

She looked up at him and he cast a pointed glance at her stomach. Her leopard growled. Seriously? He was getting all protective of her because she was pregnant? That almost made her want to put him down right then and there.

"I'm fine," she snapped. "And next time, let me handle my own business." She strode to the door and shouted out. "Les! Get some beers back here."

She turned back round to see Thunder frowning at her, but he wisely didn't say anything. Val threw herself back in her chair, trying to lounge in a way that would appear like she hadn't a care in the world, Inside, though, she was trembling. Not seething, that would have been far easier to deal with. Gabriel's words kept turning over in her mind.

There was a reason she tried her best to keep the girls away from all gang business. The same reason that her parents tried to keep her away from it as she was growing up. She knew that, like her, they would one day have to learn what it was that their mother did. She'd have to make the same choice her parents had. If they were still alive, what would her life be like now? Would she have joined the gang, or would she have been able to have an actual life?

"Just ignore that jerk," Thunder suggested to her. He sat back next to her and put a hand on her knee. "He's just a bitter old man."

His hand started to move up. Val stared at it. When her gaze traveled to Thunder's face, he gave her a pearly-white smile and cocked an eyebrow. The invitation was clear. She considered it—after all, he was far more her speed than Gabriel was. Not to mention, he was a member of the gang and he'd never hid his interest in her.

He was also handsome, in that smooth-shaven, magazine glossy sort of way. She didn't know if he oiled his skin or what, but it always seemed to glow. His eyes, dark and endless, were just the sort to let a girl get sucked in and lose all control. Maybe she should indulge. Erase Gabriel from her mind and body. It wasn't like she had any qualms about hopping from one guy to the next.

Thunder might even be willing to make it a *ménage a trois*.

She didn't want him touching her, though.

As Les brought in the beers, Thunder moved back. He nodded at her, respecting her decision, and cracked open a beer for himself. Les handed one to Val and she set it down.

"Just a soda for me, thanks."

Les's brow furrowed, but he nodded without a word.

Thunder took a couple swallows of beer and leaned back. "So, they don't know?"

"Nope." She folded her arms and glared at nothing in particular. "Don't know how Typhoon found out. I haven't told anybody yet."

"Well, your secret is safe with me."

Val laughed as Les came back in with her soda. As he passed it to her, she saw in his eyes that he had figured it out. He gave her a small smile as he patted her shoulder and left again. Some of the unease that she had been carrying around ever since she found out eased. Maybe she did have an unorthodox life, but she also had an unorthodox family. She wasn't alone in this.

Her mind trailed back to Gabriel. Why was he the first person she had told? And why did she have to spit out so many cruel words at him?

*Self-denial?*

Thunder opened his mouth, but before he could say whatever was on his mind, Jackson came in. His face was pinched with worry and Val quickly got to her feet so he could see that she was okay. He embraced her, holding her tightly, before he stepped back. He grunted as he nodded at Thunder, then grabbed a beer and sat.

"What's this about?"

"The new vampire king, Cromwell." Thunder gulped down some beer. "He had a visit with Typhoon last night. Started trying to make him hand Shadow over, but then changed his mind. Burned the contract of peace right in front of us."

Jackson snarled under his breath.

Val chugged soda, enjoying the burn of it as it moved down her throat. "He's planning on going after my girls." Just saying the words made her gut burn. "That's why I had so many of the gang assigned to go watch over your place. You remember what Astrophel said when he went after Ava? That he wanted to sacrifice her to resurrect "the master". Said he needed a kite, a panther, and a lioness. We already know that Artemis is a kite. Vampires can sense these things about shifters."

Her stomach twisted in knots and she clenched her hands. Right now, she wanted more than anything to go track down Gabriel and beg him for help. Forget about her pride and just let herself be utterly vulnerable to him. Was it because he was so sexy, or because she wanted someone to come home to at night? Someone who she could trust with her girls as much as she trusted herself and Jackson?

"You think Cromwell is going to try to hurt the girls?" Fury raged on Jackson's face.

“Yeah. And he’s going to come after me, still. Because I’m pregnant and apparently being pregnant means that he can kill me and resurrect his dead brethren.” The way Astrophel had tried to kill Ava, pregnant with Lily, to bring back his son. She stood as Jackson’s eyes widened. She didn’t want to talk to him about this, not right now. “I need some air.”

She stormed from the bar into the alley, slamming the door shut behind her. Once alone, she leaned back against the cool bricks and closed her eyes. What was wrong with her? She never lost her cool like this. She couldn’t blame it on being pregnant, either, because she knew that she could handle the hormones.

Her leopard urged her to go to Gabriel.

This was all his fault. Because he was always there when she didn't want him to be. Always there when she was feeling most vulnerable. Always there. And she wanted him. Wanted him so badly. If she asked him to, would he be her baby's father? She didn't know who it was, biologically. There were at least three possibilities and none of them men that she wanted in her children's lives.

She used sex as a drug, going back to it to relieve the pain in her mind. Hell, these days she was getting to be as big a slut as Thunder was.

She pulled her cellphone from her pocket and dialed Gabriel before she could talk herself out of it. Her hands trembled, but she held the phone to her ear. She needed to apologize to him. To tell him what was going on and bring him back, so they could tackle this thing together.

“Cunningham,” he grunted when he answered.

Val hung up at once. She groaned as she pressed her head back against the bricks. She needed her head screwed on straight… how much more could she take before she fell apart?

# Chapter Ten

*Blizzard*

Yellow tape crisscrossed over the door. Gabriel frowned grimly as he stepped into the house of the latest scene. It had been two weeks since he had discovered that the vampires were selling venom-laced drugs. In that time, the cases of 'overdoses' had nearly tripled. Even though the Brotherhood had sent a few dealers his way, he hadn't been able to weed them out.

And now here he was, at the scene of the first fatality.

From the strong wild scent in the house, it had been a shifter who succumbed. Gabriel's stomach twisted as he followed Katie to the bodies. Two people, a husband and wife, lay on the kitchen floor. Her hands were locked around his bleeding throat, a knife in his hand plunged into her chest. Both their faces were twisted with rage and horror.

Gabriel turned away, fighting the need to vomit. Not because of the scene or the blood splashed around, clearly indicating a violent struggle. It was because these two, who had pictures of a happy life together, had ended up like this. He breathed shakily, his stomach clenching.

When was this going to end?

He had put out warnings, telling the local news that there was a bad batch of drugs in the area and even going so far as to encourage people to bring them in exchange for a return of money, street value and no charges or arrests. He knew it was a long shot, but had hoped that this could be avoided. Now there were two people dead and a child in the hospital, having witnessed his parents brutally murder each other.

The Brotherhood was no help. So they had turned him onto a couple of leads. Just enough to get him to stop poking around. Just enough to make him think that they were going to be helpful. But they weren't, and he should have known better than to think that they would be. No. He needed to be more proactive. If Jackson was going to give him the runaround... well, he was going to start hauling his boys in.

To hell with Typhoon and Thunder and all the others. This was his town. People he was meant to protect. There would be no more families torn apart because of the fucking vampires. It had to end. One way or another. Today.

***

Jackson still wouldn't answer his calls. Which left Gabriel with only one course of action. He didn't like marching up to the house Jackson shared with his mate, but what choice did he have?

He knocked firmly on the door and when Ava answered, he fixed her with a severe look. "I need to talk with Tornado."

Ava pursed her lips. Her eyes flashed, but she didn't tell him to get lost as he'd expected. "What about?"

"There was a homicide linked to the drugs tainted with vampire venom early this morning. He's not taking my calls and I need to knock some sense into that dumb head of his and make him tell me what's going on with Cromwell."

Ava hissed between her teeth and waved her hands at him, as if to tell him to be quiet. Behind her, he heard the murmur of voices. Visitors? Civilians? No… As he listened a little harder, he heard that it was young voices. Val's girls. The air rushed from his lungs. Did that mean that Val was here, too? Should he confront her, force her to finally talk to him alone about what had happened? If she meant what she said, then that was it. He'd back off and they could go back to their pleasant antagonism. But he had to hear it from her, when there wasn't anybody else around for her to keep up appearances.

"Look," Ava said, bringing his attention back to her. "I get it. You're worried and you have nobody to blame except Jackson."

"That's not it at all."

"No?" Ava snorted and rolled her eyes. "And that's why you come marching up here and start banging on my door and shouting like that? Because you're *not* blaming my mate for what's happening? I don't want you here. There are other ways to get ahold of Jackson without charging up to his home and terrifying his nieces."

Gabriel bit back a growl and lowered his voice so that the girls wouldn't be able to hear. "I have tried other avenues. Jackson is deliberately avoiding me. I know there is more going on with the vampires than I've been told. I get that I'm not part of the Brotherhood anymore, but when it comes to vamps—"

"If you needed to know, I'm certain that Jackson would tell you." But there was doubt in her eyes.

Gabriel took a step back, teeth bared in a grimace. “Whatever. Just pass the message onto Jackson. I need to talk to him. Right away. Tell him… tell him I’ll give him a freebie out of it.”

Ava frowned, but nodded. Gabriel turned on his heel and marched away. He felt himself trembling. This wasn’t the first time he’d offered Jackson a ‘freebie’. The promise to do something—anything, without questions—in exchange for a single action which may or may not give him something in return. He’d done it once before and Jackson had held onto that promise for years. But this situation was worth it. He needed to know what was happening if he was going to stop it.

He needed to know.

***

He was at the morgue, sadly looking over the bodies of the victims from the previous night, when Jackson and Val walked in. They both glared at him with distrust in their eyes, but all he could manage was to nod at them in relief. At least, to Jackson. He couldn't bring himself to look at Val.

"Thank you for coming."

Jackson snorted.

"The situation is getting worse." Gabriel gestured at the two bodies. "Please... Let me help make sure these are the last two to die in whatever schemes Cromwell has."

"We can handle Cromwell," Jackson shot back, folding his beefy arms.

Frustration started to rise in Gabriel's throat. It came out as a snarl. He still refused to look at Val directly, but he could see her distrustful sneer well enough. "Vampires are the threat here, Tornado. Not me."

"I said—"

"So, when it was you against Typhoon, with your mate's life at stake, it was fine for you to call me in for backup, but now when it's bigger than one person? These two were married. They had a son that watched his parents kill each other because they were poisoned with vampire venom. This is about saving *lives*. Children's lives. Don't think I missed all the guards you had around your place earlier. You know this is dangerous."

Val looked at the faces of the dead couple and Gabriel finally allowed his gaze to land on her. She looked troubled, more so than he'd seen in a while. Dark smudges bruised under her eyes and there were premature lines making her face look years older. He took a step toward her and she drew back, threatening eyes turning on him.

"You shouldn't have called us in over this," Jackson said. "It's a tragedy, but if there was anything to tell you—"

"There is something. There is something to tell me and you're not telling me."

"We don't need help from you." It was Val's turn to speak. "We don't need help. Not from a coward who runs away and pouts when he's beaten."

Gabriel knew exactly what she was referring to. His wolf whimpered, a surprisingly submissive reaction when normally it would be raring for blood. It wanted her to listen, to understand. Bile rose in his throat, a bitter taste. He hadn't told anybody why he had left the gang. They all made their assumptions and he hadn't thought it necessary to correct them. Now, though...

"I didn't leave the gang because Jackson beat me when I challenged him for the position of alpha." He had meant to snarl it out, but it came out sounding tired. He shook his head. "I left because I knew if I didn't, I'd end up killing him."

Saying it out loud brought forward a rush of emotion. The strength of it made him reel, but he was glad to have finally said what he had been holding in for so long. He let out a slow breath, gaze flickering from Val to Jackson to see their reactions.

The two of them glanced at each other.

Jackson shrugged. "Hardly makes much of a difference, does it? We'll be in touch."

"No, you won't," Gabriel growled.

Neither of them replied to that as they walked away. Val hesitated at the door, but then only closed it. Alone with the dead, Gabriel stood growling softly. Now what?

***

Late that night, Gabriel was woken by a fierce pounding on his door. He had not been sleeping, but the noise still startled him. He got to his feet when suddenly a window shattered. His wolf surged forward, sizzling beneath the surface in case of an attack. He dropped into a crouch as a person sped into the room.

It was Val. Covered in blood, her clothes hanging in strips around her, indicating a partial shift. Her eyes were wide, horrified, and her jaw hung open. Her gaze roved the room several times before it focused on him. She skidded to a stop, panting hard.

“Val.” Gabriel moved to embrace her and she skipped back, away from him.

“They took my daughters.” Her voice was hardly more than a whisper. Suddenly she launched herself at him. Her whole body shook with sobs as she beat against his chest with her fists, not nearly at her full strength. “They took my daughters!”

Gabriel caught her wrists even as dread washed over him. “And we are going to get them back.”

Tears still streamed down her face, but Val nodded. Gabriel pulled her in close even as he started toward the gun cabinet in another room. He unlocked it and then opened the safe for the ammunition. Val, still sniffling, loaded herself up. Without a word, they headed outside again. Val slid into the passenger side of the police cruiser and hunched down so she couldn't be seen from outside.

“Where to?” Gabriel asked.

“My place.”

He nodded and headed there. From the corner of his eye, he saw Val shivering and shaking. He wanted to reach out and comfort her, but didn't know how. Eventually, she spoke.

"What did I say to you? Before Thunder arrived at the safe house. I know I said something awful. I just can't remember."

Gabriel frowned. "You said... that we only slept together because of the vampire venom. I don't recall if there was anything else."

"That's not so bad. A lie, but not so bad."

Gabriel flicked the sirens on and stepped on the gas, pushing it as fast as he dared. "Honestly what you said in the bar hurts a lot worse. Not that you care."

Val straightened. "I do care. I'm sorry. I didn't mean to say those things. Well, I meant to say them, but I didn't mean the actual words. If that makes sense. God. I'm sorry, Gabriel. I am so sorry. I don't know what's wrong with my head. I want you so bad that I can't sleep at night, but whenever I see you, it's like all this rage starts choking me."

"I hurt your brother. I almost killed him." Gabriel's shoulders sagged. "I betrayed you. It's only natural, Val. But... but it would be nice if you'd be a little more honest with other people."

She let out a shaky laugh that quickly turned into a sob. "I can't lose my girls," she cried, pressing her hands to her eyes. If I lose them... then I've got nothing to live for. I can't... I can't lose them, Gabriel. Please, please help me get them back. I know I have no right to ask you, but please—"

Gabriel cupped her face with one hand while keeping an eye on the road. "I will do all I can, Val. I will not rest until your girls are back in your arms. Now. I assume Jackson will be at your place when we get there?"

"Yes." She sniffed and rubbed her eyes. "I don't think he'll be happy that I brought you."

"Tough luck for him. He'll understand. What about Thunder?" Thcy were almost to Val's place now and he eased off the gas. Various bikes were already parked on the road and lawn. Even from here, he saw the front door smashed in.

"Thunder went back to Ivywood."

Gabriel nodded. He brought the cruiser to a halt and climbed out, Val beside him. Jackson appeared in the doorway. To Gabriel's surprise, he looked relieved to see the two of them and strode forward. He grasped Gabriel's arm and nodded.

"Looks like I'll owe you a freebie after this," he murmured.

Val laughed, once more choking on a sob. "You guys do know that sounds like a sex favor, right?"

She collapsed into sobs again. Jackson pulled her in close to his chest, his expression both fierce and at an utter loss. In this moment, he wasn't an alpha. He was a big brother whose nieces were in danger and whose tough-as-nails sister was falling apart. Gabriel waited for a beat, but his wolf was already demanding he take over, so he did. This once wouldn't hurt.

"What have you started to do?"

"I've got men out looking for Cromwell and other vampires. They picked up a trail. I also sent some others to the cave where Astrophel tried to kill Ava."

Val pulled away from her brother, face determined. "Cromwell burned the contract of peace. He declared war on the Savage Brotherhood. He wants to reclaim vampire supremacy and Artemis can shift into a kite. He wants to sacrifice them to bring back 'the master', whoever that is. He's not going to be dramatic like Astrophel was, he'll have taken them into the heart of the mountain, so he can be assured of victory."

Gabriel stared at her. His brain reeled from the information. That changed... *everything*. This wasn't an attack on Coalfell anymore, this wasn't about the Brotherhood wiping each other out. His wolf snarled, hackles rising. He wanted to shout at them both that this was information they ought to have given him before, but he made himself stay quiet. They should have told him, but that was beside the point now.

"Then the best way to get them back will be to infiltrate the vampire kingdom itself."

Jackson ran a hand through his hair, eyes wild. "We'll die if we try."

"If we rush in like an army, yeah," Gabriel agreed. "But Val is called Shadow for a reason and I'm pretty good at stealth. We go in alone."

Jackson opened his mouth, but Val interrupted. "Yes. We go in alone."

He closed his mouth again. His shoulders sagged. Gabriel could see he wanted to protest, but it was a credit to him and how well he knew his sister, that he didn't. Val reached for his hand and gave her brother a small smile. Fear shone from her eyes, but it was quickly being consumed by determination.

"No matter what happens, I am going to make sure my daughters get out of there alive."

Gabriel's wolf whimpered. He reached out before he could stop himself and brushed his fingers against Val's stomach. If he listened hard enough, he could almost hear the beating of her unborn child's heart. He wanted to tell her to stay behind. To not risk herself or her child. But her daughters were in danger and he knew the only thing that could stop her from going after them was death.

"Get *all* of your children out," he murmured. He'd die if he had to, but she had to live.

Val pressed a hand over his. She met his gaze. "My girls are our first priority. No matter what else, they get out. Even if it means you leave me behind. Otherwise, I'll kill you myself."

A surprised laugh bubbled up his throat. Without stopping to consider that Jackson was still watching them, Gabriel leaned forward. He brushed his lips against Val's and she threw her arms around his neck. The kiss was passionate, desperate and full of things neither one could say. When they broke apart, Jackson looked like he had been slapped.

"Didn't see that coming," he mumbled, then his face hardened. "When you get back, we'll have to have a long talk about this. Now get going."

"Yes, sir." Clutching Val's hand, Gabriel raced back to his cruiser. Time was running out.

## Chapter Eleven

*Shadow*

The cloying scent of vampire venom mixed with the buzz of cocaine made Val's ears itch. She and Gabriel had rolled themselves in the tainted drugs to help mask their scent as they infiltrated the mountain. Though she hadn't purposefully breathed any of the drugs in, there was a certain amount of transfer that was bound to happen.

The entrance to the vampire's kingdom was easy to find. The scent of them was strong around the cave mouth and grisly skulls were carved into the opening. They slipped inside, and it soon became apparent that either this was a trap, or Cromwell wasn't expecting anybody to attempt this. There was hardly anybody here. Once they'd killed a couple of vampire guards to find the path clear, Val started to get uneasy. What if they were in the wrong spot?

They continued on, until the low murmur of voices reached them. Then Gabriel suddenly reached out and grabbed her arm.

Val looked around for a trap, but the wolf's eyes were only on her. His grip tightened as he spoke in a low voice. "Before we go and probably get ourselves killed, there is something I need to tell you."

What the hell was he doing? "We don't have time for this, Blizzard."

A look crossed his face, but she didn't know what it meant. "You can kill me later. My wolf wants you. It has for a long, long time. It's more than mere lust, Val. It wants to be with you always, and it hurts every time you look at me with hatred. If we get out of this, then I think there might be a possibility that you and I are—"

"Stop." Her leopard urged her to take his words and reciprocate them, but her heart pounded, and her head spun. This was the worst possible time for this conversation. Not when they didn't know what they were going to find. "We don't have time for this, Gabriel. You can pour your heart out when we get my girls out of here."

He nodded once, and then leaned in. Her leopard pleaded with her to accept the kiss, to lean into it and pledge herself without words to him. Instead, she reared back and punched his shoulder, putting distance between them again. What was he thinking? Was it the cocaine? Maybe she should have come alone, if he couldn't keep his mind focused on their mission.

"Time for the mushy stuff later," she hissed, moving once more through the tunnels.

The murmur of voices grew louder. They came to the end of a tunnel, where light was pouring in from the room on the other side. Her heart pounded as she reached for Gabriel's hand. Cromwell's voice came through the murmur, but what exactly he was saying, she didn't know.

And suddenly she couldn't leave it as it was between them. She glanced at Gabriel. "I'll fuck your brains out once my girls are safe."

She darted forward, just hearing his low chuckle. "You'd better."

As soon as she got to the opening of the tunnel, Val saw why they hadn't run into very many vampires. They were all gathered in the room below. She cursed under her breath; they were a good hundred feet up from the floor. There were other tunnels branching out lower, but none at floor level. Clearly a defense against shifters. All vampires could fly; but how was she meant to get down there?

Her heart nearly stopped when she saw her girls. They were tied up in the center of the room on a large wooden platform. Bundles of sticks were placed around them as Cromwell chanted in a language she didn't understand.

If she jumped in, there was a ledge there and there, she could jump from them and then onto that tapestry and then onto that ledge and then—

Gabriel grabbed her arm and dragged her away from the edge. She hissed at him, but he ignored the unspoken threat until they were at a fork in the tunnel. Then he grasped her by the shoulders and narrowed his eyes at her.

"We split up. Find different ways to get in that don't involve making a hundred-foot death leap. Find a way in, closer to the ground, and wait for my signal. Don't go in prematurely unless there isn't another choice. Understood?"

Val rebelled against the orders, even though she knew it was her best chance. She swallowed down the need to be in charge and nodded. Gabriel charged off down the new tunnel and she backtracked to the last branching and went down that one. She didn't bother with stealth, moving as quickly as she could. She'd be able to trace her way back with her own scent.

Her heart raced as she found another opening into the main room. This one was only about ten feet from the floor. She crouched in the shadows. From this angle, she could see that her girls were all struggling weakly. Freya's head was on Artemis's shoulder. Drugged. Fury rose up in her, but she held herself back, waiting for Gabriel's signal.

Cromwell's chanting suddenly stopped. His head swiveled to look right at her and he started to laugh. "Well, if it isn't Mother dearest. Come out of the shadows, Valarie. You're not fooling anyone."

Val bared her teeth, but leapt from her hiding spot. A surge of satisfaction swept through her when the vampires nearest her backed away. Maybe she was losing her touch, but at least they still feared her. She walked forward like she owned the place.

"Let my girls go and I won't kill you," she told Cromwell.

He laughed again. "Do you really think that frightens me? You, alone in a hall of vampires? Even if you kill me, my people will simply resurrect me. No. Your girls... they're special. My Master, the first vampire and a god that walked among mortal flesh, will be returned to us through their sacrifice. You should be honored; they will be greatly blessed in the world to come."

"If your master was a god, then how did he die?" she spat, edging closer.

There were vampires all around her. There was no getting out of this alive, not for her. Was Gabriel in position yet?

"You can ask him when he walks again." Cromwell smiled. "I am glad you're here. The blood of your unborn child will strengthen him once he has arrived. And now... light the pyre."

Everything seemed to stop at that moment. Her head swiveled to see a vampire stepped up to the platform her girls were tired to. A flaming torch burned in his hand. Val let out a scream of pure hatred and sprang at him. She batted the torch away as she shifted. Her teeth tore into the vampire's throat and ripped it out.

A howl made her smile, but she didn't slow as she rolled over the torch, putting it out. Then she sprang to her feet and charged at Cromwell. He shifted to the balls of his feet and opened his arms, as if to embrace her. Val twisted herself around, shifting back to human form to kick the vampire in the chest. He grabbed her leg and she shifted back to her leopard form, using his momentum to claw at his face.

The chittering call of Artemis in her kite form distracted her. She turned her head to see Artemis beating her wings, her red-gold feathers gleaming in the pale light, as she dug her talons into Freya's arm, trying to lift her. She just saw Gabriel seize Sekhmet around the waist and all but throw her to one of the openings, then kick a vampire in the face, before Cromwell's arms wrapped around her throat.

Val choked, clawing at his arms. Cromwell squeezed tighter. Freya shifted into a red-gold lioness and scrambled up after Sekhmet as Artemis flew after them. Gabriel turned and caught her eye. A look of dread filled his expression. Then he shifted, sprang after the girls and disappeared into the tunnel.

*Good.*

Cromwell shouted something, but Val didn't listen to his words. She closed her eyes, drawing the anger and hate from deep inside her. Her leopard snarled, and sound cut out around her. When she opened her eyes again, everything was in shades of red. She tore herself from Cromwell's arms. Vampires were going after Gabriel and the girls.

She leapt onto the back of one, snapping its neck, before going after another. She disemboweled that one before swiping her claws across the throat of another. One lunged for her neck and she caught its face in her jaws and clamped down, crushing bone. The taste of blood was sweet, and her leopard took over. Clawed open another vampire. Tore the head off another. She quickly lost track of the body count as she killed vampire after vampire.

A roar filled her ears and Cromwell rammed her body. The force sent her flying through the air. As she landed, the sound of her heartbeat filled her ears. It stuttered, allowing the hummingbird beat of her unborn baby's heart to fill her ears. The red faded from her vision as she crouched. The girls were out; she needed to get herself out now. She sprang for a low tunnel, but even as her claws scrambled at the loose opening, Cromwell was there. His nails grew to daggers and he stabbed them into her flanks.

Val twisted, slashing at his face, but he dragged her back, too quickly for her to reach him. He threw her away from him. She skidded to a stop near the pyre. Blood tasted on her tongue and poured down her flanks. She crouched low, her ears flattened against her skull as her eyes darted around the vampires surrounding her.

She was going to die. That was okay. But she was damn well going to take as many of these bastards out with her as she could!

"A mother's instinct," Cromwell muttered as he stalked toward her. "It will make your blood all the sweeter for my master."

Val sprang for him again. He met her with a backhanded blow; as she was flung away, though, Cromwell stumbled. A howl filled the room and there was Gabriel, his wolf's form huge and beautiful, as he tore into Cromwell's back. The other vampires lunged for him and Val sprang to her feet. Pain lanced through her body, but she ignored it as she hit a vampire hard in the back.

*Where are the girls?* She wanted to demand of Gabriel, but there was no chance. As another vampire came at them, he released Cromwell and blocked its path. He barked at Val, jerking his head towards the tunnel.

She froze. She couldn't leave him. Couldn't—

Another howl. The roar of a lion. A bear's grunting charge. From all around, members of the gang streamed in. The vampires shouted and attacked. Fur and blood flew in the air as Val retreated. The pain was so bad she could hardly see. She panted, foam at the corners of her mouth. Everything seemed to spin around her as she closed her eyes. It was only now that she felt the fire in her veins; she'd been bitten. More than once, if the weakness in her muscles was any indication.

She forced her eyes open again. The gang was outnumbered. They'd take out plenty of vampires, but there were more pouring in from every tunnel. Cromwell stood in the middle of the pyre, trading blows with Jackson as he shifted from wolf to human and back to wolf. Val's head spun. There was no retreat here, not for the Brotherhood—only a fight to the death.

Unless they found a different way.

Val threw herself into the fighting as Jackson lunged for Cromwell's throat. The vampire slashed at him with dagger-like fingers. He was too late, though. Val's teeth sank into his arm, yanking him off balance. Jackson pinned him to the floor and went for his throat.

"Stop," Val shouted as she shifted back to human. She grasped Jackson's shoulder as he growled. "Trust me." Jackson narrowed his eyes, but nodded. He kept the vampire pinned as Val got to her feet. She spread her arms wide. "Your king has fallen once again!"

Her voice rang through the fighting. At first, she didn't think it would make a difference, but then she saw the vampires disengaging. Within a few moments, the shifters had formed a circle around the pyre, facing outward at the vampires. The scent of blood was so strong in the air that it choked her. Val stood tall, spinning on her heel so she could look at all their enemies.

"Take a look at your dead brethren. Think about all those who have already died. The Savage Brotherhood might not win this battle, but we will exact a heavy toll on your numbers. We are not divided, and we will kill every single one of you—unless something gives." She glared down at Cromwell. "Unless a new contract of peace is written up, you die today."

Cromwell snarled at her, hatred burning in his eyes.

Jackson shifted back to human form and jerked the vampire to his feet. "Your choice, vamp. Death or a new contract. You'll be telling us how to save the people you poisoned, too."

The vampire's face twisted into a smile. He lifted his hand, reaching to swipe across Jackson's throat. Val leapt forward. Before she could reach them, though, another vampire, this one slightly shorter than Cromwell, was suddenly there. He wheeled Jackson out of the way, then deftly snapped Cromwell's neck. The vampire glared at the others as Cromwell's body dropped.

"There has been enough death," he called, pulling himself up straighter. "We all knew that Cromwell would only lead us to oblivion. I declare myself the new king and I will give you your contract." He turned a glare on Jackson.

"So long as shifters leave us to live, we will do the same for you."

Jackson narrowed his eyes, but nodded. Val grinned—then her knees buckled, and everything went black.

***

The next few weeks were hell. There was enough venom in her system that in the few moments when Val was lucid, she was certain she was going to die. At times, she wanted to die. It was only the hummingbird heart low in her belly and the sound of Gabriel's voice in her ear that kept her from succumbing.

Eventually, though, the sickness passed. When she woke, she found that the new vampire king, named Kristoff, had drawn up a new contract of peace with Typhoon. He had ceded land to the Coalfell chapter and was working with the other vampire kingdoms to find a more sustainable way to survive other than drinking human blood.

He hadn't revealed the secrets as to how the vampires were able to walk in daylight now, but that hardly seemed to matter. Not when there were so many other limits on them.

Val kept out of gang business while she recovered. It was nice, being at home with her girls every day. She'd had to explain to them about the vampires and what the Brotherhood did, but they seemed to be taking it well enough, considering. None of them wanted to stay in their house or sleep in their own beds and she found herself with Ava and Lily constantly. It didn't matter to her, as long as her girls were safe.

When Sekhmet started to complain that Freya had gotten to shift before her and she was younger, Val knew that they were going to be okay. She was still worried about this business of 'the master', but vampires could no longer cross the border without being disintegrated within a few minutes, so they were safer than ever before.

Which only left one loose thread.

Val ran a hand over the fresh buzz she had gotten and nodded at her reflection. She'd elected for softer makeup than she usually went for—when she bothered to wear makeup—and the leather jacket emphasized her curves. A fresh tattoo, covering an ugly scar on her hand, gleamed in the light. She smiled and left her room.

“Girls,” she called and held out her arms for her daughters as they rushed to her. “Be good for Auntie Ava and Uncle Jackson.”

Jackson, who had Lily and was bouncing her gently, frowned. “Where are you going?”

She winked at him. “To claim my mate.”

## Chapter Twelve

*Blizzard*

Gabriel typed the last few words of the report he'd be sending up the ladder and glared at his computer. It had taken him some time to figure out exactly how to explain the strange happenings around here without mentioning vampires. Now that he was done, he knew that this was going to stir up a lot of shit. At least as far as the Brotherhood was involved. It would be so much easier if he could just get Typhoon to pull some of his state-level strings to have the incident brushed under the carpet.

The only thing that gave him any sort of satisfaction was the fact that they hadn't lost anybody else to the tainted drugs. That new vampire king had kept his word, and everybody who had been on them was now recovering. No shifters going rabid, no humans turning into vampires.

*Maybe Jackson will speak to him on my behalf. He did say he owed me a freebie.*

The door opened. He looked up and only grew tenser when Val came in. Her hair was freshly buzzed and... were her lips pink? He didn't have much of a chance to stare because she marched over to him and slammed her hands on the desk. Her breasts strained against her leather jacket, cleavage bursting from the top.

"We have to talk," she said.

The fierce grimace on her face left no room for argument, even if Gabriel had been planning on it. He slowly stood, reaching for the cuffs on his belt.

"You're right," he said grimly. "There are still charges on file against you and—"

Val rolled her eyes. She practically leapt across the desk, grabbed his collar and brought her mouth to his. Heat flared through him instantly. He wanted to let himself get swept away by the ocean of passion as it passed between them. He hardened just with the eagerness of her kiss. But he knew it couldn't be.

He cuffed one hand and, as Val pulled back, gasping, he cuffed the other. As she blinked in surprise, he quickly dragged her to the cells. He had to get this done before he changed his mind. His heart fluttered rapidly, and his wolf snarled, as if it wanted to tear out his own throat. What choice did he have, though? She was a criminal. He was a cop. There were more than vampires between them.

As he shoved her into the cell, Val giggled. “I didn’t think you were into bondage.”

He turned to her, mouth open to tell her not to play games, only to see her unbuttoning her jacket.

There was nothing but a fancy, blood-red bra underneath. Gabriel’s jaw dropped. He stared at her breasts, which seemed a lot bigger than they had been before, as she slid the leather jacket down to around her elbows. Then she settled herself onto the bench and opened her legs, a clear invitation. A sexy smile pursed her pink lips.

“You’re serious?” he asked incredulously.

"Aren't you?"

Gabriel stared for a moment longer before he uncuffed her. "Right. What I said before. That was just adrenaline talking, Val. My wolf wants you, but it would never work. We're just too different, not to mention I'm a cop. How would that look to the Brotherhood if we started sleeping together? Besides, I have enough on my plate without people thinking I'm dirty."

"Being 'dirty' is exactly what's on my mind." She shrugged off the jacket altogether and reached for his shirt. "Look. None of it matters. The gang, your job, the fact that we fight like cats and dogs—literally—because here's the thing. You are my mate. We're meant to be together, no matter what."

Gabriel's breath caught in his throat. "Your mate?"

"Yes." Val gave him a wicked smile as she unbuttoned his shirt. "And I intend on letting the world know it. Loudly and very often."

She licked a tattoo on his chest, eliciting a moan. Gabriel would have liked nothing more than to just let himself get swept away with the sensations, just like his wolf wanted. But this was far more complex than two people wanting each other... wasn't it?

He closed his eyes as she tugged his shirt out of his pants and greedily explored him with her hands and mouth. His skin felt too tight and he forced himself to step back. To think about this.

"If I'm your mate," *I am*, his wolf sung, "and you are my mate, then we need to figure this out. First, would you leave the gang for me?"

"In a heartbeat." There was no hesitancy in her answer. Her eyes glowed as she moved a little closer. "I have, for a long time, wondered what I was doing with my life. I know that it'll be hard, but I would leave the gang. Not just for you. For my girls. I don't want them to grow up like I did... always afraid of the day when I don't come home."

Gabriel pulled her closer, his mouth seeking hers. "Then it sounds like you've already made your decision."

Before their lips could meet, though, Val suddenly yanked back. Gabriel froze. Had he pushed her too fast? He started to release her, but her fingers curled into his shirt, pulling him back. His wolf snorted, confused, but Gabriel smiled and nodded, giving his mate—his heart sung just thinking of it—time to process her thoughts.

"You don't just get me," Val warned him. "If this really happens—"

"It's happening. You're my mate."

Her eyes widened, then a smile burst across her face. It was the purest, most radiant smile he had ever seen, and his heart fluttered just looking at it. She pressed herself to her toes to kiss him, then completed her thought. "You're becoming an instant dad, too. A father of four."

Gabriel nodded. His heart was so full, he didn't think it could get any fuller. "Of course. Val, I love them already. Why else do you think I could leave you behind to get them out of the vampire's mountain?"

Tears suddenly pooled in her eyes. Val laughed a little, then buried her face into his shoulder. "Thank you."

Gabriel held her close, knowing that there were no words for this moment. Well… perhaps three words. "I love you."

Val's arms snaked around his back and she turned her head to start kissing his neck. God, he was going to have to work to keep up with her. "Love you, too."

Her breasts pressed against his naked chest as Val's kisses sent chills down his spine. With a small growl, he ripped his shirt off the rest of the way and pulled on her jeans. They slid off her hips, revealing she was utterly naked beneath. As his hands grasped her ass, pulling her closer again, he nipped her shoulder. The gasp of pleasure was all he needed to encourage him to continue.

He ran his hands up the soft skin of her back, feeling the slight ridges of scars that she had hidden with tattoos. He let his fingers linger on each one as her hands sought out his own scars. They pulled away from each other, foreheads brushing as their hands explored each other's bodies, finding each and every hurt that they had suffered. Val pressed her hand flat against one of his ribs, onto the scar he had gotten the day he had almost killed her brother.

"I knew that was why you left," she whispered. "I knew. I think that's why I hated you so much. Because you were meant to always be there and then... I had to hate you, but I still wanted you to be with us."

Gabriel ran his thumb over a crescent moon on her breast that covered teeth marks. "Is he going to be okay with this?"

"He'll have to."

Val looked up at him. Her eyes so big and beautiful, sparkling. Such tenderness and vulnerability in them. It took Gabriel's breath away, even as she undid his belt. He stood, letting her have control as she kissed her way down his twitching abdomen and pulled his jeans down with her. She settled them at his knees, then grinned up at him while she took him in her hand.

His head fell back as she stroked him, increasing the need inside of him, while at the same time relieving some of the aching pressure. His wolf growled in pleasure, content to be tended to. He tucked his hands behind his back, letting his eyes drift shut. Whatever tension had been in his body to this point slowly released, replaced by a different type of tension. He was already hard when she took him into her mouth, but the warm wetness made him swell even more.

His hands clenched together as she sucked, moving her head slowly to give him maximum pleasure. There seemed to be a fire in the pit of his stomach, glowing hotter every time her lips came to his end and then slid back down his length. Gabriel concentrated on breathing evenly, although he couldn't stop his periodic groans.

One of Val's hands ran up his thigh, making him tremble. She laughed softly, then did it again. This time she left him long enough to kiss his hip and make her way down his thigh, her free hand still stroking him.

"I think it's time you sat down," she moaned breathlessly.

Gabriel wanted nothing more than to have this continue. Except for two things. He kicked off his jeans, aching to be inside of her. But when he pulled her to her feet and guided her so she was sitting now, he didn't enter. Not even when she opened her legs invitingly.

He knelt before her and her eyes widened. "Aren't you ready?" she asked, looking concerned.

"More than ready." He cupped one breast in his hand, finding the nipple beneath the fabric of her bra. "I want you to be ready, too."

"I..." Her face colored.

Gabriel rose a brow at her. "Don't you want me to suck on your clit? To ease my fingers inside of you while my tongue moves in circles, until you're feeling so tight you might burst open? So that you're slick and swollen, ready for me to enter?"

Val squeezed her free breast in her hands, panting. The scent of her arousal made him grin. "Yes, of course, I do... but I thought that you'd..."

His wolf growled. She thought he'd be selfish about it, did she? He kissed up her thigh and then back down to her knee. "Did I just shove myself inside of you at the safe house?"

"No."

“Then why did you think I’d do it here?” He brought her knee up over his shoulder and glared at her in challenge.

Val chewed her lip, then relaxed. She laid back on the bench, pillowing her head with one arm. “Guess it’s just one of those things. We’ll get to know each other as time goes on, right?”

Gabriel nodded and moved in, so he could lick her clit. “Can I be on top this time?”

A shiver ran down her spine and he grinned, loving the way her eyes rolled into the back of her head. Her mouth dropped open and she gave a little moan. He repeated the action, then pushed in deep so he could suck on her clit. It was already hard and swollen, the perfect size for him to wrap his lips around. Val clutched at the bench beneath her as he did his work. The points of her nipples stabbed up into her bra so hard, it was a wonder they didn't tear right through.

When she was shaking, her hips rocking with every move he made, he repeated the question.

Val held her arms out to him. "Yes."

He eased a finger into her, finding her ready and mounted her. Her legs circled his waist as she stared up at him, so much trust and love in her gaze that it took his breath away. He entered her slowly, making sure that she was ready every inch of the way, while her back arched and a satisfied sigh escaped her.

Gabriel started moving, letting his body and hers find a natural rhythm together. It quickly grew into a frenzy, both thrusting hard together. He leaned over her, capturing her mouth with his, while her fingers tangled in his hair. Soft cries burst from her throat, over and over, filling his ears with her sweet music.

He ground his teeth against his arousal, wanting this connection to last forever. His hands tightened on her hips and her fingers tugged the hair at the back of his neck. The combined sting and pleasure nearly sent him over the edge, but he held on, his eyes never leaving her face. Her chest, neck, and cheeks flushed red as her head fell back. A cry tore from her, then another as she clenched around him. He forced himself to ride her orgasm out and when another rocked her, he allowed himself his own release.

Gabriel collapsed over her. Their bodies stuck together with sweat as they breathlessly kissed again and again.

After some time had passed and they were laying quietly in each other's arms, content to cuddle on the narrow bench, Val turned to him. She traced her fingers over his lips and a small smile crossed her own. When she slipped one of her fingers into his mouth, he eagerly gave it a gentle suckle. Val sighed and returned to tracing the shape of his mouth.

"I love you," she said softly.

"And I love you."

She grinned and rose herself to one elbow. "I don't think I'll ever get tired of hearing you say that, you know. You love me."

"You'd better hope I do, since we're mates," Gabriel teased. He winked at her, then grew serious. "So. Do you think that this means we ought to get married?"

"Married?" Val laughed. "Are you serious?"

Gabriel nodded.

Her laughter died, only for her grin to widen. "Oh, I see. You want the excuse to put me in some frilly white dress that you can tear off with your teeth, don't you? We don't need to get married for that. We're mates. We love each other. What do we need some piece of paper for?"

"Well... it will make things easier."

"What things?" Val cooed. "Taxes?"

"No. I mean… adopting the girls."

Her eyes widened.

Gabriel gauged her reaction for a moment before he eased himself a little to the left, so that they could look at each other better. "I am going to be their father and I want it to be official. So that if anything happens… I know you said you're leaving the gang, but I see death all the time. I just want to make sure everything's in order… I mean, as long as it's what you want."

Tears pooled in her eyes as she nodded. "I want you to be their dad. So, yeah, adoption sounds great." Her hand drifted to her stomach, which was just starting to round out with pregnancy. "Is it legal to put your name as the father on the birth certificate even though we know you didn't sire her?"

“I don’t know. I’ll look it up.” He pulled her close again, a feeling of warmth and contentment rushing through him.

This was all he wanted from life, to have his mate in his arms and the excitement of getting to know his children. His wolf stretched and snoozed, for once lazy and not feeling the need to go out and dominate everything. He stroked Val’s stubbly head as he considered what their future would be like. He’d remain sheriff, so he could continue to help people the best way he knew (unless, of course, Val wanted him to quit—then he’d find some other way to do it). He knew Val would end up bored as a stay-at-home mom, but there was so much she could do. Open a bike repair shop, start teaching self-defense classes, go back to school.

He hugged his mate to his chest and grinned. The possibilities for their future were endless.

*****

THE END

30549403R00151

Printed in Great Britain
by Amazon